Shamus
in a
Skirt

Maggie Sullivan mystery #4

M. Ruth Myers

Published by Tuesday House

ISBN-13:978-0692556290
ISBN-10:069255629X

Cover design by Alan Raney

ALSO BY
M. RUTH MYERS

– Maggie Sullivan mysteries –

No Game for a Dame
Tough Cookie
Don't Dare a Dame

– Other Novels –

The Whiskey Tide
A Touch of Magic
A Journey to Cuzco
Captain's Pleasure
Friday's Daughter
Costly Pleasures
Love Unspoken
An Officer and a Lady
Insights
A Private Matter

ACKNOWLEDGMENTS

As always, I am indebted to
the Dayton Police History Foundation
for its excellent collection
of photos and information
on Dayton policing through the years.
Any inaccuracies are entirely my own.

I am also deeply grateful
to the Tuesday House editors
for their thoughtful suggestions,
which made this a better book.

Lastly, I want to thank
the loyal readers
who have followed Maggie Sullivan
through her adventures.

.

ONE

I was balanced on the radiator in my office, using the butt of an automatic to hammer one end of a sagging window shade, when the war that was starting in Europe crossed the Atlantic to peek up my skirt.

The gun hadn't functioned for some time.

Neither had the shade.

Neither had our miserable excuse for a building manager.

At this rate, I figured F.D.R., who was coming to Dayton in a couple of weeks, was more likely to stop by and get the shade working again than the lump downstairs who'd ignored three requests. I gave the roller spring a final smack as the door behind me opened, followed by a low whistle.

"Holy smoke, that's a fine pair of stems you've got!"

I looked around.

A round little guy with his hands in his pockets beamed up at me. His checkered suit was two shades short of being flashy enough for the vaudeville stage, but nicely made. Puffing a stogie, he unrepentantly admired the length of my legs.

"You gotta be Maggie Sullivan." Halting, he rocked on his heels. "Word is your detective work is as good as your legs, and I wanna hire you. As of now." He brought out a billfold. "Whatever you're working on, drop it. I'll pay twice your going rate. Plus expenses."

Weighing the temptation of a double rate against his obnoxiousness, I dropped down from the radiator. My visitor grinned at me. I was five-foot-two. He came to the bridge of my nose.

"People with manners knock before they come into an office. Feel free to go out and try it. Second, ditch the stogie if you want me to listen. Third, people I don't know generally introduce themselves when they come looking to hire me."

Lines that looked like delight formed at the edges of his eyes. He didn't speak. Stuffing the billfold back under his jacket, he turned and ambled out.

I wouldn't have bet two cents he'd return.

I wasn't sure I wanted him to.

Was I nuts? More than a month had passed since I'd had anything beyond routine clients whose fees paid the bills but didn't allow me to squirrel anything away for emergencies. My DeSoto needed new tires. I'd taken to riding the trolley except on Thursdays when I needed the car to drop off my laundry.

I put on my shoes and went back to my desk. Pretty soon the shoes would need resoling too. As I sat swiveling from side to side, and maybe wishing I hadn't jumped on my high horse quite as fast, there was a knock at the door.

"Come in," I said with as much cordiality as I could muster. It wasn't much.

Mr. Checkers reappeared, still beaming. His bouncy gait telegraphed energy disproportionate to his size. He doffed his hat and gave a snappy little bow that made me dislike him less than I should have.

"Joshua Tucker, impresario *extrordinare* turned purveyor of elite temporary accommodations," he announced grandly.

The nuns at Julienne had all but buried us under vocabulary lists. I was fairly sure *impresario* had something to do with managing dancers and comics and such. The theater, anyway. It would explain his oversized confidence. And the flashy suit.

"You own a hotel," I translated, concentrating on what he'd indicated he did currently. "Either that or sell those trailer homes people are supposed to tow behind their cars."

He grinned from ear to ear.

"You're a corker. That's okay. In fact it's better than okay, because I'm in a jam and I need help. If I insulted you complimenting your legs, I apologize. I used to hire a lot of dancers — how I met my wife, as a matter of fact — so I can't help noticing.

"Anyways. Will you at least listen to why I need you?"

I sighed inwardly. To his credit he'd recognized I'd found him offensive. Some men were oblivious. And I had to admit, there'd been an innocence in the way he'd looked at my legs.

"Why don't you sit down, Mr. Tucker?"

"Joshua. I use the whole thing. Maybe to balance out the guy that goes with the name being short."

He pulled back the chair in front of my desk and sat. It gave me a chance to make closer assessment. Mid-forties. Dark brown hair, still plentiful and neatly cut.

He started to set his hat on my desk, then thought better.

"Okay if I put this here? I got a bad habit of walking off and leaving them if I use a hat rack."

I nodded. Nobody was likely to mistake him for upper crust, but other than the suit, maybe even including the suit, he had a certain polish about him. Under his breezy manner, I now could see he was worried.

"Tell me about your problem," I said. "Then I'll decide if I can help you."

"Okay." He puckered his mouth up as if hunting where to begin. "It's got to do with jewelry. The high-class kind. Know what I mean?"

3

"Diamond bracelets and such?"

"That's it. I think some might have gone missing in my hotel."

For a moment I wondered if I'd misunderstood.

" 'Might have'?"

"Yeah." His fingertips patted his knees. Left-right, left-right, left-right. He watched me, all traces of his earlier exuberance obliterated by tension. He didn't seem inclined to say more.

"Look, if something's been stolen, you need to talk to the police," I said.

He already was shaking his head.

"You don't understand. Our hotel — mine and my wife's — it's exclusive. Small. Twelve suites and twelve rooms. The people who stay with us want privacy. It's part of what they pay for, and they pay plenty. Most of the women travel with jewelry."

He halted without seeming aware that he'd done so. I'd seen it before in people who couldn't bring themselves to put into words what they would then have to face as reality.

"And?" I encouraged. I understood about his guests having jewelry. What still wasn't clear was his comment that some *might* have gone missing. "Mr. Tucker? Joshua? I'm assuming you have a decent safe where your guests can leave valuables."

He blinked, recovering.

"Sure. Better than decent, too. Supposed to be top-of-the-line. Last night, though, I was having trouble sleeping. Figured I might as well go downstairs and see to some paperwork, so I dressed and went down to the office.

"And I know what I'm gonna say now sounds silly, but you know that feeling you get sometimes? Like something's not right?"

The thing was, I did. On more than one occasion it had alerted me to trouble. Maybe saved my life. I nodded.

"Well, I walked around. I noticed the dial of the safe wasn't quite where it should be. I told myself it was probably nothing, but I decided to have a look, just for peace of mind. So I opened the safe and shook all the boxes and one didn't rattle. When I looked inside, it was empty. But this morning when I looked again, it wasn't."

TWO

He lost me then, talking a mile a minute without making much sense. I needed to calm him down. I opened the bottom drawer of my desk where I kept the fixings for gin and tonic. Joshua Tucker looked like he needed one, and it would have been inhospitable to make him drink alone.

"Let's back up," I said when we'd held conference with our glasses for a minute. "I want to make sure I'm getting this straight. Last night you opened every jewelry box in your safe and one of those boxes was empty."

"Yeah."

"This morning you opened them all again. They all contained jewelry."

"Yeah."

"How do—?"

"We keep a list of what goes in and out, see. Last night the cases in the safe matched the ones on the list. This morning I counted again. Same number of boxes. All of 'em full."

The guy was on his toes, I'd give him that. Questions popped into my head faster than I could think. I pictured jewelry boxes I'd seen in stores. In the places where I shopped, they'd hold a nice watch or a strand of pearls, not the rarefied valuables he had described. My guess was the outside would look almost the same, though.

"The boxes you're talking about are black velvet, right?"

"Most. A couple are dark blue."

"Then how can you be certain the box that was empty last night was in there this morning?"

For the first time since he'd started telling me about the jewelry, a small smile returned to his face. He edged forward with eagerness.

"That's easy. It's got a little place near the back corner where the color's bleached out. Owner probably handled it right after she'd dabbed on perfume, had some residue on her fingers. Or it could be that some kind of makeup left a smudge and her maid tried to clean it off with something she shouldn't."

It was possible my would-be client had spotted something from dumb luck. Or it could be an explanation worked out in advance. But why? Why would he make up a story like this? Why would he offer to pay me good money?

Tucker had tipped his head to the side. He was watching me closely.

"So, these questions mean you're gonna help me?"

It still sounded like a matter for the police. It was also as far removed from the sort of case I normally handled as the office where we sat sipping gin was from China. There was something else, too. That instinctive warning of something amiss that Tucker had mentioned didn't occur unless you were already half expecting trouble, or doing something you shouldn't be.

"What else made you look in the safe last night?" I asked, leaning forward.

The question startled him. He tugged at an earlobe.

"Nothing. I don't think. Unless...." He shook his head as if to clear it of an unwanted thought. "Five or six days ago, when I opened the safe for the first time that day, the dial was a little off too. Not as much as last night, though, so I didn't even think.... That must have been somewhere in my brain when I noticed last night."

"You keep saying the dial wasn't where it should be. You don't leave it on the last number after you open it, do you?"

"Never. We spin it a couple of times, then set it on the number of the day. That changes. Only it's never on the number exactly. One day it's just off the number, the next day a quarter off, next day it's halfway to the next number. Then that part repeats."

Not a bad little system.

"Who besides you knows the combination? The whole procedure?"

"William, our manager. Been with us from the beginning. And of course my wife. I'd trust either of them with my life."

"So someone could have been in the safe after you. Apart from our presumed thief."

"But they weren't. Like I told you, we keep a log. Besides, nobody checked any jewelry out last night. Only things in or out yesterday were Count Szarenski getting his passport and bringing it back several hours later, and right before I went upstairs for the night, a new arrival putting two cases in."

My thoughts had stumbled to a halt when I heard the word 'Count.' I stared at the round little man in front of me. I wondered if I should revise my initial assessment of him, and whether his establishment bore any resemblance to the picture taking shape in my mind.

"How do you know the cases the new arrival put in weren't empty?" I managed to ask.

"They were the dark blue I told you about. The one that was empty last night was black." He edged forward again on his chair. "Look, I've got to get back. Have I told you enough? Will you find out what's going on?"

"Mr. Tucker, I still think you might be better off going to the police—"

"And I already told you, that's not an option. Our reputation ... if guests get even a hint of something wrong...." Unable to finish, he spread his hands. "And some of them, the last thing they need to see right now is police. That Polish count and his family have been through plenty. Jump at the least noise. And a cable just came, pretty garbled, but I think we're supposed to expect a woman whose husband got killed when the Nazis took Paris."

Until now, tanks in Poland, and even the bombs that had started to fall on London two weeks ago had been only newspaper headlines. Now a war half a world away was casting its shadow clear into Ohio.

"You gotta help." Tucker kneaded his thumbs. "We've got insurance, but it might not be enough, and if jewelry got stolen, the scandal would ruin us. We'd — we'd lose the hotel. We've put everything we have into it. Ourselves into it. Losing it would just about kill my wife."

He owned a fancy hotel. I rented a rundown office where one of the window shades wouldn't go up. I'd never tackled a case like the one he was outlining, and there were things about his story that bothered me, but I knew what it was to pour your entire being into a dream.

"I'll have a look around," I said. "One day, maybe two. Until I get a feel for the problem, that's all I can promise."

He bounced to his feet, happy as a kid.

"Thanks. Thanks more than I can tell you." He flourished his billfold. "You haven't told me your rate yet. How's fifty sound for a starter? Plus all your expenses."

"Extremely generous, Mr. Tucker."

"Joshua."

"Joshua."

"Here's what we'll do then. You'll check in like the rest of the guests. No charge for the room, of course—"

I held up a hand.

"Joshua. You just told me you've got a count staying there. Rich people. People traveling with pieces of jewelry worth more than I'll earn in my lifetime."

"Okay?" He looked puzzled.

"My dad was a cop. My only nice jewelry is a strand of pearls I got for high school graduation. You can't honestly think you'll pass me off as one of your guests."

9

His shoulders gave a crestfallen slump.

"If you just come in asking questions and they learn you're a gumshoe, it's going to upset them as much as the cops."

"They won't know I'm a detective. I'll be somebody working for you."

"Doing what?"

"I'm not sure yet. I need to see your setup first, get a better sense of the problem. What time can I come by tomorrow?"

"I thought you were going to drop everything."

"Those were your words. This is the best I can do."

I nudged his retainer forward, inviting him to reclaim it.

"Half-past eight in the morning. Have breakfast with Frances and me in our suite."

"It's better if you and I are the only ones who know what I'm really doing."

For the first time since I'd met him, Tucker glared.

"I don't have any secrets from my wife."

I stood at the window and watched him leave and wondered what was bothering me. What was wrong with earning a fat fee on a case which, as an extra enticement, didn't sound likely to result in cracked ribs or stitches?

THREE

Friday morning, five minutes early, I sashayed into The Canterbury wearing my best suit. It was dove gray wool suitable for all but the hottest days of summer. I didn't have any fancy jewelry to spiff it up, though I did have a stylish little semi-automatic I sometimes used on occasions too dressy for my Smith & Wesson. I hadn't worn either today. The Canterbury didn't seem like the sort of place where someone might try to shoot me.

The hotel sat on a side street, just far enough from the center of town to be discreet. It was brick and four stories tall, small but quietly elegant with its royal blue awnings. A doorman with enough gold braid on his uniform to lead a marching band kept order between the entrance and the passing world.

"Miss Sullivan!" The hotel owner bounced forward to meet me before I was two steps inside. "Hey, thanks for coming so early." He pumped my hand. "It'll give you a chance to meet Franny and see the lay of this place before things get busy."

His face shone with enthusiasm. He'd traded his checkered suit for a striped one today, but any improvement was marginal. Talking a mile a minute, he whisked me toward an elevator whose polished brass practically blinded me. I had no chance to so much as look at the lobby.

"You're going to love Franny," he promised as the Negro operator closed the grill of the elevator and the car started up. "She's smart as they come. Don't know what she ever saw in a mutt like me."

We stopped on the top floor and stepped out onto thick Axminster carpeting.

"We're the one at the rear." Tucker gestured. "Nice and quiet. Nobody going by. Franny and I had spent so much of our life in hotels, we thought we might have trouble getting used to anything else. We put two suites together, so we have a pretty nice setup."

With obvious pride he threw open the door to a light-filled living room. A stunning redhead stood with her back toward us and a telephone pressed to her ear. At the sound of the door, she turned, smiling warmly. She was leggy and tall and I figured her husband's head would come about to her shoulder. She was one of the most attractive women I'd ever met.

"I'm afraid I must go. Yes, I'll tell him. 'Bye," she said with the rushed cheer of someone trying to end a conversation. Shaking her head in apology, she came toward us with an outstretched hand.

"I'm delighted to meet you, Miss Sullivan—"

"Maggie." She had a nice handshake.

"Maggie, then, and I'm Frances. I was rather afraid Joshua might send you running."

"I have a way of putting my foot in it sometimes," he said, gazing up at her affectionately.

"With girls, mostly, so I'm generally glad." Her elbow nuzzled his shoulder. "Breakfast just arrived. Let's sit down before it gets cold."

"Who wants you to tell me what?" Her husband nodded toward the telephone.

"Oh, Miss G's in a snit because one of the scrub women didn't come in last night."

An oval table sat in an alcove formed by a bay window at one end of the long living room. The furnishings of the room, from chairs to landscape paintings to whatnots, looked as if they'd spent a couple of generations in an upper-crust home. Frances seated herself by a serving cart where she lifted silver domes from dishes of eggs, ham, sautéed mushrooms and such. My usual morning fare was oatmeal, but I managed not to turn up my nose.

"I don't suppose you've had any thoughts yet on the mess we've got on our hands," Frances asked as soon as we had food and coffee. She tucked her cap of coppery hair behind her ear. "Sorry, that was silly of me. Of course you don't when you haven't even started. It's just that I've been in knots...."

Tucker reached across the table and patted her hand.

"Hey, kid. Everything's going to be okay."

Her laugh was wobbly. "If I had a nickel for every time you've told me that!"

"And I've been right, haven't I?"

She nodded and dabbed at her eyes.

They were as mismatched a pair as I'd ever seen: her looks and his, her refinement and his rough edges. I wondered if the affection they displayed was genuine. And mutual.

The warmth of Frances' greeting had seemed genuine, but the more I saw of it, the more I felt certain her bright animation was an effort. To put both of them at ease, I asked how they'd chosen the hotel name and how they'd met. When someone's in trouble, learning about their past is always a smart place to start.

The hotel, as I'd surmised, was named for Chaucer's wandering pilgrims. Tucker had been a kid performer on the vaudeville stage. From there he'd become an emcee, then a theatrical manager specializing in dance and variety acts. One day Frances had shown up for an audition.

"I just about cried when he hired me to fill a chorus line vacancy," she said. "I was two weeks behind in my rent and a day away from being tossed out on the street. Although the street might have been better than the cockroaches skittering through that wretched room."

She nudged food around on her plate but had eaten nothing except a teaspoon of eggs and some nibbles of toast. Either she was off her feed or she was nervous.

The couple's theatrical work had taken them everywhere: Chicago, Milwaukee, San Francisco, even London. In between, they'd spent time in New York. But they'd grown weary of travel. They knew more successful touring performers and show executives would welcome a hotel that offered a bit of luxury and a lot of privacy. Dayton's location on the main east-west rail line and good connections everywhere, made it ideal.

"It's pretty clear the two of you have made a lot of friends through the years," I said once they were talking freely. "What I'm wondering is, have you made any enemies along the way?"

They both stared. After several seconds their gazes slid uncertainly toward each other.

"Well, I suppose I've ruffled some feathers," Tucker said. "Like I told you, I kinda put my foot in things sometimes—"

"I'm talking about more than ruffled feathers. Someone you fired, for instance. Jealous boyfriends. Girls who wanted you to represent them, but you turned them down."

"There were probably lots of guys who were sore when I married Franny. She's a knockout. And girls I wasn't sold on enough to represent?" He shrugged with palms turned up.

"But no one stands out? No one's ever threatened you?"

"No," said Tucker.

"No," echoed Frances. "No, never!"

A thread of shrillness infected her voice.

"What about—?"

The knock at the door was loud enough to startle us all.

"Oh dear, I'll see what it is." Frances jumped up.

"What about since you opened the hotel?" I asked. "Has anyone—?"

"No. I have to see him now!" a man's voice insisted.

"Oh, for crying out loud," Tucker muttered. He threw his napkin down and rose.

Wondering whether the argument might prove instructive, I moseyed after him. As Frances moved aside, I saw a man in the black attire that waiters in fancy places wore.

"Whatever the problem is, Pete, it'll have to wait," Tucker said sternly. "I'm talking business here. I'll be down in ten minutes."

The waiter shifted nervously.

"I'm sorry, Mr. Tucker, but you need to come right now. You have to."

"Why?"

The waiter swallowed. His eyes skipped from me to Tucker and back again.

"Well, come on. Spit it out."

"There's a policeman at the back door. They've found a - a body. In one of the garbage cans. Somebody said they thought she worked here."

FOUR

"Polly. Her name was Polly."

The missing scrub woman. The one somebody in housekeeping had been complaining to Frances about on the phone earlier.

"I never learned her last name. She only started here two weeks ago, or thereabouts," Frances said.

She sat with her arms on her knees, rolling a china teacup back and forth between her hands. The two of us were alone in her apartment.

Tucker had asked me to stay with her while he went to meet the policeman. More than an hour had elapsed before he reappeared to tell us it was the woman who hadn't come in the previous night. He didn't know the three women who worked late at night as well as he knew other employees, he explained. Since this one was new in addition, he hadn't been certain enough to identify her. The head of housekeeping, the one the Tuckers called 'Miss G', had viewed the body and confirmed it.

Now Frances and I were on our own again. Tucker had gone back down to inform key members of his staff what had happened and see to it rumors didn't start spreading.

"She was just a kid," Frances said, rolling the teacup. "Seventeen, eighteen." She gave a shaky laugh. "I suppose I ought to be grateful it wasn't one of the guests, but—" She looked away, blinking tears into her lashes. "Do you think

— will the police come around asking questions? Lots of them, I mean, talking to everyone?"

"I don't think so," I said, mostly to reassure her.

Her husband's report had been rushed. Other than the fact she'd worked here, the police didn't seem to be looking at any connection between the dead girl and the hotel. What he'd told us next was plenty for me to know they would be.

"They say it looks like someone attacked her to, uh, violate her." He'd looked at his shoes in embarrassment. "That killing her was just — you know. To shut her up."

It was going to be a homicide investigation.

"They'll probably talk to the woman you said is in charge of housekeeping. The one who identified her," I told Frances.

"Miss Gumm."

"They'll need to question her and some of the other employees. They'll want to establish the last time anyone saw Polly."

I wanted to know too. Had the girl died on her way to work, or as she was leaving? Miss G had been in a snit because Polly hadn't shown up last night. That suggested she'd died sometime between leaving on Wednesday and arriving last night, Thursday.

If Polly had been killed on Wednesday, it raised possibilities I couldn't sift through while making conversation with a woman I scarcely knew. Wednesday would make it the night Tucker insisted he'd seen an empty jewelry case that later refilled itself in his safe.

If the two events were connected, it also would mean we were dealing with someone more dangerous than a con artist pulling a jewelry scam.

Frances set down her teacup and started to pace, arms hugging her waist. Even with strain showing in every line of her, she was a glorious creature in motion.

"My husband is a good man," she said, her voice wavering. "He doesn't deserve this. We've worked so hard, and things were going so well. Then that wretched man disappeared, and then the safe — if Joshua's right, which he usually is — and now... Polly.

Her pacing had taken her to windows next to the dining alcove. They looked out over rooftops and, despite taller buildings here and there, gave a fine view of the Great Miami flowing in the distance. Frances leaned against the window, staring out.

"What man disappeared?" I asked.

Frances turned to look at me in disbelief.

"Joshua didn't tell you? No, I can see he didn't." She came back to join me. "Joshua gets so caught up in what's happening now that, well, it's not that he forgets the past, he just lets go of it. The bad parts, anyway." Her lips curved softly.

"And this man...?"

"Was a guest. About three weeks ago, I think. Sorry, I... was out of action for awhile, so I'm a bit fuzzy on when.

"Anyway, he was a guest. He disappeared without checking out. He'd paid in advance, so it wasn't a matter of skipping. The maid noticed when his bed wasn't slept in for two days. His things were all gone, except for an envelope he'd left in the safe."

In the safe. The part of my brain that connected things tingled.

"Did you notify anyone?"

"The police. We didn't like to, but it was so odd it made us uneasy. They sent two men. In plainclothes, which we appreciated. They looked at his room, but they said there wasn't anything suggesting a crime."

"What about the envelope?"

"They took it."

"Did they open it?"

"Not around us."

Frances went to the table. She picked up a piece of cold toast, smearing it thickly with butter and jam.

"It's too much, isn't it?" She chewed resolutely. "Three things going wrong, one after another."

"It's hard to swallow as coincidence," I agreed. As I started to ask her again about people who might hold a grudge against her or her husband, he bustled in.

"Police are talking to people who knew her. There's not many, since she was so new and worked nights. The only two times she came in the day was to pick up her pay. It's got things upside down, though, with people pulled away from their jobs to answer questions, or told to come to the kitchen 'cause they're next in line. And they're using Miss G's office — the police are — so you know how that's going over.

"I gotta pitch in where I can to keep things running. Just wanted to let you know what's happening. Need anything?"

"No." Frances stood up, licking her fingers. "Joshua, what can I do?"

"Not a thing. Just get some rest. And don't worry."

I winced at the savagery with which Frances bit into the last chunk of toast.

"Before you go," I put in quickly, "Are any of your current guests people you'd met before? You said some of your clientele, if not a lot of it, comes from show business people."

The two of them looked at each other.

"Veronica Page," said Tucker. "She used to be a pretty good dancer before she got snagged for Hollywood."

"Joshua was already managing her when he took me on. We — Veronica and I — worked in a couple of shows together."

"Has she stayed here before?"

"No. But Veronica's okay." Tucker grinned. "Cynical as they come, but decent."

"And we'd crossed paths with Loren Avery a time or two," said Frances. "Stayed in the same hotel once, I think. Didn't we all take the same ship back from London, too? Yes, I'm sure I remember talking to Loren when I was having my morning walk around deck. The ship was rolling, so not many people were out. He joked about dancers being used to dipping and bobbing. They've never stayed here before either."

Tucker's short form was rocking from foot to foot.

"I gotta get back," he said. "If I think of anybody else we already knew, I'll phone up."

"I suppose the coffee is stone cold by now," Frances said when he'd left. She tried some and made a face. "If I could look at the register, I might spot the name of somebody else we've bumped into. But it's check-out time now, and if there's a dither on top—"

"It can wait til things settle down. What would help me now, though, is finishing what I was asking when we got interrupted by the news about Polly. Can you think of anyone who might have it in for your husband? Or maybe just want to scare him a little?"

"No." Frances shook her head vigorously. "You've seen what he's like. He's exasperatingly enthusiastic, but he's sweet. He's kind. He's one of the smartest men I've ever known." Thrusting a handful of coppery hair behind her ear, she gave a thin smile. "Most men think they're smart when they're not. Joshua thinks he's not, when he actually is."

Either she actually loved the guy, or she was trying awfully hard to make me think she did.

"Could your husband be in some kind of trouble you don't know about?"

"No."

"Does he gamble?"

"Absolutely not!" Her voice tightened. "I know my husband, Miss Sullivan. I *know* my husband."

* * *

Everyone lies. It started on the day Eve nibbled the apple.

That knowledge hammered at the back of my head as I took my leave.

In the years since I'd hung out my shingle, plenty of spouses had told me they didn't keep secrets from each other. It never turned out to be true. Sometimes they told white lies, which they didn't count. Sometimes one was wrapping the other's eyes in six layers of wool.

I wondered which was the case with the Tuckers.

Frances was too upset with me to get anything useful from her at present. With the cops confining their questioning to the kitchen, my chances of leaving the hotel without bumping into one who recognized me weren't likely to get any better.

I got into the elevator still thinking about other situations where people had sworn they didn't hide anything from each other although they did. It didn't necessarily indicate a desire to deceive. One might think they were shielding the other from something unpleasant. Regardless of motive, it mucked things up when they were in trouble and had hired me to help.

Thinking through the morning's events in the quiet of my office held great appeal at the moment. But before the elevator came to a complete stop in the lobby, I heard what sounded like a first-class donnybrook.

FIVE

"What's it to you where I go and when?" a dark-haired man was snarling as I stepped out. He stood not half a dozen feet inside the hotel door with his back to the street. It seemed fair to guess he had just entered.

"It's the kind of thing somebody has a right to ask when they've waited over an hour to order breakfast." A woman with an athletic build and a tawny, shoulder-length bob faced him, blocking his way. Her outfit was right out of Vogue, but the round black frames of her specs gave her a Bolshi look.

"Can't the Queen of Sheba eat by herself?" sneered the man. "I went for a walk. Now get out of my way."

The shove he gave her had force enough to topple someone shakier on her feet.

"How dare you use that tone with me!" Instead of giving way, she caught his arm and pivoted to face him like an enraged lion.

The fury tensing the lines of his body was out of proportion for someone having a spat with his wife, or maybe girlfriend. His hand rose to strike her. Forgetting my need to remain inconspicuous, I started forward.

The woman sneezed. Volcanically. A hand caught my sleeve.

Another blast followed the first.

"Lena Shields," whispered a voice in my ear. The edge of my vision caught Frances' tall shape behind me.

In a futile attempt to cover her nose, Lena had released the man. He stepped back swearing.

"Who's he?" I murmured over my shoulder.

"Boyfriend." Frances moved to my side.

"Very attractive." Jerking his handkerchief out, the boyfriend dabbed at his cheek. He had looks enough to turn women's heads, slender, with smooth, even features and a mockery to his mouth that probably fluttered the pulses of some. "I thought I told you to pour that perfume down the drain."

"It's not the perfume," Lena snapped.

"Like hell it's not. You bought it a week ago, and you sneeze every time you wear it."

"Then maybe you should buy me some that suits me better. Oh — that's right, you can't afford it." Her words were acid.

Having produced her own hanky, Lena dabbed her nose. She stalked toward the elevator. At the reception desk, departing guests who had paused to watch returned to settling their bills. The angry boyfriend made for the hotel's small bar. I heard him order whiskey.

"Gee," I said to Frances. "Not exactly my idea of two love birds. Do you know all your guests by name?"

"I try. Those here more than a night or two, anyway." She laughed nervously. "It sort of goes with the job."

She smiled at a passing member of the hotel staff. "I thought it might help if I came down and made myself visible while Joshua's busy with the police. Make things look normal. I'm glad I saw you. I wanted to apologize for being so weepy. And for being rude when you asked me things I know you had to ask—"

"You weren't." A party of three came in the elevator. We moved further out of the way. "If things settle down here today or you need me, I'll be at my office. Otherwise, I'll come back tomorrow."

So far, I hadn't seen anyone I recognized as a cop in the lobby. A quick peek out one of the heavily curtained windows didn't reveal any uniforms unless I counted the doorman.

Eager to make my escape and sift through all that I'd learned and observed that morning, I stepped outside. And swore softly.

* * *

Across the street where he could watch all the comings and goings from the hotel, a man with a halo of red-gold curls above a cherubic face sat grasshopper-like against a storefront. A Speed Graphic with a flash on the side and other camera equipment hung from his neck. Deluding myself that I might somehow escape his eagle eye, I started quickly toward a gravel parking lot two doors down.

"Morning, Mags!" Cheerful as always, Matt Jenkins caught up with me. "One of the Hollywood luminaries got themselves in a pickle already, huh? What is it? Blackmail? One of them light-fingered? Spill."

A bell in my head jingled. Tucker mentioning a guest who'd been a dancer before she went to Hollywood.

"I have no idea what you're blathering on about, Jenkins."

He was a shutterbug for the afternoon paper. At the moment he was the last person my clients needed hanging around.

"Uh-huh. You were just in the mood for breakfast here instead of the dime store." Behind gold-rimmed specs his eyes twinkled.

"It's a high-class place. The owner hired me to run a background check on someone they're thinking of hiring."

"Hogwash."

We'd been friends too long. We knew each other's ploys. Sometimes we shared information the other wanted, extracting tit for tat. Sometimes we couldn't.

It wasn't making me happy that Jenkins seemed better informed about The Canterbury and its guests than I was.

Since he had me at a disadvantage, and knew it, the one thing he wouldn't expect was for me to act like it was just the opposite.

We'd reached my DeSoto. Hoisting myself onto the hood, I gave a satisfied smile.

"Bribe me."

For once, I'd caught Jenkins flat-footed.

"What?" His gaze sharpened.

Jenkins was as smart as they came. Dealing with him was like dealing with the brighter sort of criminal. You doled out minimal information yourself in hopes they'd tip their hand enough you could use a crumb or two that fell out.

"The Canterbury is as private a place as you'll find. Their guests place more importance on that than they do on room service," I recited. "Anything I give you will be pure gold. I'm thinking six months of credit, minimum. Plus a steak dinner and the Carousel."

We kept an informal tally of favors. At the moment I couldn't recall which of us owed the other. The terms I'd just proposed were so outsized that Jenkins bobbled between doubt and drooling.

"It *could* be blackmail, like you said. Or it could be scandal," I tempted.

I needed to throw him off. And I needed to find out more about the Hollywood people he'd mentioned.

"Instead of movie stars, think European royalty," I said. "Where'd you hear the nonsense about movie people? I hope you didn't pay good money for it."

"My sources are more reliable than yours, and mine don't go to jail. This guy's never led me wrong."

"Yeah? Who is he?"

Jenkins wagged his finger.

"Nice try, Mags."

He was regaining his stride.

"Probably some star-struck clerk from City Hall. So eager to see a live actress, he mistakes half the beautiful women he sees for one."

"As a matter of fact, he works at the train station. He's how I got word that horn player from the Benny Goodman band had slipped into town."

Jenkins, his wife and I went to hear jazz together when we had a chance. On the occasion referenced, we'd gone across the river to a Negro club on West Second where we squeezed in to stand at the back. Our reward had been breath-taking playing for an audience that had learned of the event by word of mouth. I filed the prospect of a source at the depot away for later exploration.

"Well, this doesn't have anything to do with Hollywood starlets," I said, and hoped it was true.

Jenkins didn't jump in to correct me that it was somebody major, or give any names. Nevertheless, I'd learned something, and I'd managed to keep the nature of my client's problem — or problems, now that a body had turned up as well — confidential.

"So," I said. "Do we have a deal?"

His eyes narrowed.

"Do I look crazy enough to fall for those terms? Give me something to whet my interest and I'll owe you three — count 'em — three rounds of information." He held up three fingers.

Out on the street, a police cruiser passed. Knowing Jenkins might see it, I waved brightly. He scarcely looked before his attention returned to negotiations.

"*If* you don't hang around, waiting to snap pictures." I tried to think of other end runs he might pull. "And you don't sic one of your reporter pals on it."

"Where's my down payment?"

"Veronica Page." I hoped I'd gotten the name right.

"Veronica Page!"

His face came alive. Apparently the name meant something to him. Jenkins went to picture shows a lot more than I did.

"She's not a star, but she's been second lead a time or two. Who else?

It was my turn to waggle a finger.

"Stick to the deal, and who knows what kind of chance I might throw your way."

"Okay for now, but I expect more. Oh, and Ione said invite you for dinner tomorrow if I ran into you."

He started away, walking backward. The police car was safely out of sight around the corner. Possibly parked in the alley though, and no telling where Jenkins' route now would take him. I hopped to the ground.

"Where are you headed? I'll give you a ride."

SIX

I was at my desk eating a turnip when the head of homicide came calling. I'd picked up the turnip at the produce market down the block from my office.

It was half-past one, and considering the substantial breakfast I'd had at The Canterbury, the turnip made a fine lunch. Its peelings were piled on a used envelope at the edge of my desk, a salt shaker was at hand, and I'd just cut off a nice slice when the door opened. A cop named Freeze walked in with two of his men trailing him.

"Lieutenant Freeze," I said. "Always a pleasure."

He frowned, not sure whether I was being polite or being a smart ass. I wasn't sure either. Freeze was lean, with a hard face that went with his job and a pretty little nose that didn't. His two assistants lounged obediently against the wall.

"Turnip?" I offered him the fresh slice. It bought me an extra three seconds to choose my dance steps.

"One of our officers saw you leaving The Canterbury hotel this morning," he said, ignoring the turnip.

"Glad to know there's nothing wrong with his eyesight." I raised my eyebrows, mutely inquiring his point.

Freeze exhaled as if counting to ten. He didn't like me much, but I'd proved myself a time or two when he and his team had dropped the ball. A jittery truce existed between us.

"What were you doing there?" he asked with barely reined annoyance.

"They've hired me to do some work. Background checks on people they're thinking of hiring, like I do for Rike's department store and other places."

My bread and butter work.

In my last, hurried confab with Tucker, I'd told him to give that explanation in case any cops who knew me saw me there. Now I was glad.

Freeze narrowed his eyes.

"A place like that does a lot of hiring?"

"Don't know. I haven't started. The owner was getting ready to spell out details when somebody ran in telling him he had to come, that the cops had found a dead girl in the alley."

It seemed like a waste to let a good slice of turnip dry out. I popped it into my mouth and chewed, then talked around it.

"I assume that's why you're here?"

"You're a swell detective."

He'd planted himself in front of my desk, and stood with legs spread and arms crossed, ignoring the chair available for visitors. I'd recited my piece about why I was at the hotel, yet he wasn't leaving. It made me uneasy.

"Gee, Freeze, I hope you don't think I can tell you anything useful about her, because I can't. She worked nights. Scrubbed floors, I think. The woman in charge of housekeeping was on the phone when I got there, grousing to Mrs. Tucker that the dead girl hadn't shown up for work last night."

Freeze hadn't had a cigarette hanging out of his mouth when he entered, which unusual. He remedied the situation, watching me closely.

"Just checking all angles. Looked like the girl had been pretty. Maybe the boss had discovered she could do something other than scrub."

"Did you meet his wife? Mrs. Tucker?"

"Boike talked to her."

Boike was one of the detectives with him. He was fair haired and built like an icebox.

"A man with a wife like her would have to be nuts to philander. Right, Boike?"

He looked up from taking notes, which seemed to be his usual assignment with Freeze. At a glance from his boss okaying comment, Boike nodded. The burly detective actually did have a voice. I'd heard him use it when he was on his own.

"Funny he'd fire a man for making a pass at the dead girl then, don't you think?" Freeze asked.

Had he guessed he'd catch me off guard? I stretched, determined not to let him win a round, and irritated Tucker hadn't mentioned firing someone when I asked about people with grudges.

"What I think is, all those years he managed theater people taught him to get rid of troublemakers," I said. "Freeze, if you were any more off on this, you'd be on the moon."

But I was worried. If Freeze believed there was even a grain of truth in what he was saying, he could have men sniffing around the hotel for days. That included talking to guests. Joshua Tucker could end up without a soul getting wind of his jewelry problem only to see his hotel destroyed by unfounded suspicion related to something else.

"It just seems like a strange coincidence, you showing up at a place linked to a homicide," Freeze said.

"The only link is the girl worked there. You going to tell me there haven't been any other girls raped and killed in this city?"

"How did—?" He clamped his mouth shut, aware too late that I might have been guessing about the rape, which he'd just confirmed.

"Look, I know you're just doing your job," I said, switching tactics. "Checking every possibility, like you said. How about hunting a connection between the dead girl and the man who went missing from the hotel a month or so back?"

A muscle twitched in his jaw.

"Is that what butterball hired you for?"

"I already told you why he hired me."

"Yeah? Well, why ever he did, you've got yourself a client who's crazy as a bedbug. Either that or he made up the whole thing about a man disappearing."

My mouth opened several seconds before I found my voice.

"Why would he do that?"

"Maybe to make it look like someone's got it in for him. To deflect suspicion when he does something else he's planning. Say, killing a girl who didn't appreciate his advances or was making demands or—"

"Get out."

"Then he fancies the whole thing up by hiring a shamus in a skirt that he can buffalo."

I rose, clenched fists grinding the desktop to keep from punching him.

"Get. Out."

* * *

To sweeten the sour mood left by Freeze and the fact my client had omitted useful information, I went for a walk along the Great Miami. It wound through the heart of the city, creating a hairpin bend before heading south to empty into the Ohio. Clouds slow waltzed in the brilliant end-of-September sky. A man in much-patched trousers flew a homemade kite accompanied by delighted shrieks from two tykes trailing him.

Why hadn't Tucker told me he'd fired someone when I'd asked about people who might have grudges against him? It could be, as Frances had said, that he got so caught up in the present he put past events out of his mind. Or it could be deliberate. Whatever the reason, he'd gotten himself into more trouble rather than less.

My client was an odd little duck, but Polly's murder convinced me he hadn't imagined the tampering with his safe. Or, despite Freeze's skepticism, invented the tale of a missing guest. Unfortunately, Freeze now suspected him of murder. I had to punch a hole in that theory before I began hunting what lay behind Tucker's trio of problems.

What did I have to work with?

Freeze's slip of the tongue had confirmed that the dead girl had been raped — or it looked as if she had. He'd also said she'd been pretty. Had Polly been more than pretty? It would open up explanations for her death beyond an affair with her boss.

More interesting still was Freeze's use of the past tense. It *looked like she'd been pretty*, he'd said. That implied she no longer was. It conjured two possibilities. One was that her face had been beaten, or maybe slashed with a knife. The other was that she'd been strangled.

The question of when the girl had been killed also niggled at me. Sitting with Frances that morning, I'd learned the night scrub women came in at midnight. The late-shift dishwasher was getting off then, as was the bartender who presided in the small lounge, and maybe a couple of others. With employees coming and going through the back kitchen door, it was hard to imagine anyone being attacked and killed just beyond it without being noticed.

On the other hand, only three women cleaned in the hotel at night. At half-past four in the morning, they were the only ones leaving. The city wasn't yet stirring with milk deliveries and bakers' trucks. The alley would be deserted.

Polly hadn't made it to work Thursday night. That meant she'd either been killed while arriving at midnight, which seemed unlikely, or while leaving work Wednesday — the same night Joshua Tucker had noticed suspicious activity in the in the hotel safe.

SEVEN

Finn's was the closest I had to a home after selling the one I grew up in to pay my dad's medical bills. Scarred tables and mismatched chairs gave the pub a comfortable, lived-in feeling. Framed photographs of donkeys pulling hay carts and Irish countryside decorated its walls.

"Maggie's here. She'll do it for me, since all you cops are too yellow," said a jockey-sized man at the bar as I entered.

"Only thing yellow in here is your leg," observed one of the regulars.

"Keep a distance," another warned me. "He smells worse than usual."

"I'll do what?" I asked.

Two fruitless hours at the library searching old newspapers for articles on The Canterbury had left me in a bad mood. Now it lifted.

"Shoot a dog that peed on me. Just look!" Wee Willie Ryan thrust out a leg. A damp spot of unmistakable origin spread from knee to cuff of his letter carrier's uniform.

"Willie, if he'd known you better, he'd have bitten you too," I said solemnly.

The crowd along the bar hooted with laughter. They'd have been disappointed if Wee Willie and I hadn't scrapped. The two of us had gone all through school together up until high school. Individually and together we'd set records for getting in trouble.

I slapped the top of Willie's shoulder as I moved past. He was nearing the end of the single pint he had before going home to his wife and kids.

Amid a goodly number of cops who had just come off duty, two white heads stood out. I'd been hoping they'd be here. The brushy one topped a stumpy form. The one with silvery waves accompanied a craggy face and bony body. I made my way toward them.

"You want a stool? You look kind of peaked," said Billy, the short one, assessing me critically.

The two of them and Billy's wife were my godparents. Billy's favorite pastime was being a worrywart. Rather than waste breath trying to reassure him, I slid onto the offered stool.

"What I want, is to ask you two gents what you know about a hotel called The Canterbury."

"That the one used to be The Prince Regent?"

"And before that, Hotel Linden-something," said Seamus. "Lindenwood, that was it."

Billy nodded. They'd been my father's best friends. What they didn't know about the city wasn't worth learning.

"I think it's gotten to be a pretty tony place these days," said Billy. "Some fellow came in and bought it five or six years ago when things were rock bottom bad. Poured a lot of money into it. Fellow from the East, is what I heard."

Seamus nodded. Seamus wasn't much on talking unless he had something he thought needed saying.

Five years earlier, when I'd left my floorwalker's job at Rike's department store to set up shop as an investigator, I'd outlined some boundaries between us. I didn't expect inside information from them — nothing they wouldn't tell anybody else, I'd said. In return, I didn't expect them to seek information from any case of mine beyond what I volunteered. The arrangement had worked, and I honored it now.

"I don't want you telling me anything you shouldn't," I said cautiously, "but the guy who owns it wants to hire me.

He wants me to evaluate their security. I thought I'd better check with you two before I rushed in. Make sure the place was on the level."

Billy practically popped his buttons. It was exactly the sort of prudence he longed for me to show. Seamus eyed me with a glint of skepticism. I didn't like misleading them, but technically it was true. A hotel's security included a safe.

Finn's wife, Rose, brought me a Guinness without being asked.

"Tell Finn he needs to buy a radio so people can hear the World Series this time," she said.

For the second year in a row, Cincinnati was playing. Last year, a number of regulars had abandoned Finn's in favor of a pub where they could listen to the games. He'd groused at the time. Now he snorted.

"Not worth it if Cincinnati loses as fast as they did last time," he said from his spot at the taps. "You just want me to get it so you can listen to that Charlie McCarthy fellow."

"Why? I already hear one dummy talking day-in day-out." Rose swept past him to a chorus of laughter.

When we were alone again, Billy and Seamus and I drank some stout.

"Any trouble The Canterbury since the hotel changed hands?" I asked.

Billy looked at Seamus, who shook his head. A bad knee had put Seamus mostly on desk duty these days. He heard things Billy didn't. They'd been partners for years, several of them after Seamus recovered from the bullet that damaged his knee. Then arthritic stiffness had begun to set in.

"No women taking strangers upstairs. No gambling or donnybrooks I've ever heard of," said Billy. Seamus nodded.

Their report made Joshua Tucker's rash of trouble even more intriguing.

We yakked and sipped and Billy left for home and dinner. I was fixing to ask Seamus if he wanted to go somewhere for a blue plate special when his gaze shifted and his bony face softened.

I knew without looking around who had entered. For one thing, I felt a jolt of energy hit the room. For another, Rose, who was mostly a solid and sensible woman, glided swiftly down to fuss over wiping our end of the bar. It put her in perfect position to greet the only customer I'd ever known to make her giddy as a girl.

"Hiya, Connelly." I turned a smidgen on my stool to nod to the cop with brick brown hair who'd come to join us.

Mick Connelly was in his early thirties. He had a casual air that hid nerve and hardness born of coming of age amid Ireland's political violence. He must have raced home the minute his shift ended, for he'd already changed from his uniform to street clothes.

"Traveling, are you?" asked Seamus, nodding at the worn valise he carried.

"On my way to the train station. I knew you'd seen the telegram come for me, and I didn't want you to worry."

"Not bad news, then?"

Connelly's face split into the widest grin I'd ever seen on it.

"Anything but." As if in a toast, he raised his valise. "I'm off to Chicago to bring back the love of my life."

Rose's eyes widened. A frozen moment passed before her features moved toward a scowl. She stole a glance at me as I sat dumbstruck.

Connelly had done everything to create the impression I was the love of his life. I'd tried to convince him I didn't want to be. I wasn't cut out for a cottage and kids. Nonetheless, I felt as though I'd just been punched in the stomach.

"Have a good trip," I managed to say. "Hope the pair of you will be happy."

"Over the moon happy — guaranteed." He touched my shoulder lightly. "We'll have a pint together when I get back, eh? See you, Seamus."

He turned to throw Rose a wink, which always fluttered her pulses, but she'd huffed down to join Finn at the taps.

Connelly strode out with his loose-limbed gait shaped by country roads. Every step sang of eagerness. I couldn't tear my eyes away.

"Well! Did you ever?" sniffed Rose, rejoining us.

I shrugged.

Seamus was looking at me. He tucked his head and smiled. It indicated what would have been a chuckle in most people.

"What's funny?" I asked, more crossly than I intended.

"This old world. The people in it, mostly."

I pushed my stout away. I couldn't swallow it. All I wanted was to go someplace dark and curl up in a little ball to stop the hurt.

EIGHT

Once Polly's body turned up, I'd told Tucker I'd go along with his plan that I stay at the hotel. The cleaning girl had been killed at night. The odd activity in the hotel safe had occurred at night. I needed a feel for the rhythm of The Canterbury and its people around the clock.

Tucker's insistence that I hide why I was really there didn't sit well with me. Neither did the prospect of being on my good behavior twenty-four hours a day. Nonetheless, late Saturday morning, resplendent in my second-best suit and a tweed hat peppered with blue and pink, I strode into the lobby. I carried a suitcase more dog-eared than Connelly's, a clipboard, and a wooden carpenter's ruler with one end unfolded.

At the front desk a woman with a little black poodle yapping under her arm was checking out. A few steps away, her maid held the woman's furs and directed a wizened bellman as he shuttled a mountain of luggage from the lobby to a waiting car. The creamy leather suitcases didn't interest me, but when I spotted a stack of hatboxes I nearly drooled. The bottom two matched the luggage, but the one on top was hot pink pasteboard decorated with a flamboyant signature: *Schiaparelli.*

Elsa Schiaparelli. The genius. The ultimate.

When I looked up, the maid with the furs was eyeing my single suitcase as if detecting the odor of something dead. I gave her a big smile.

"Is this place okay? I thought I'd try it a few days while they treat the place I live for bedbugs."

She drew back so quickly she collided with her employer, who frowned at her and trotted off, cooing to her doggie. I stepped forward.

The clerk was in his late thirties with a hint of self-importance.

"May I help you?" His eyes lifted not to me, but to someone behind me.

"Yes, please." A woman brushed around me, leaving a discreet and expensive trail of Joy. "We're checking out. If I could get something from the safe?"

"Of course. First door on the right. I'll let Mr. Tucker know you're coming."

He picked up the phone as she trotted away. I leaned forward to give my name and ask him to let Tucker know I was here, but a man who'd enjoyed one or two too many good meals charged toward the desk like an irate elephant. He brandished a telegram.

"You!" he bellowed at the clerk. "When did this get here?"

I jumped to the side, sparing my toes a trampling as the man shoved in front of me.

"It just came, Mr. Clarke," the startled clerk answered. "The bellman took it up to your room, but your maid told him you were at breakfas—"

"You got a phone down here that can make a connection to Cuba?"

"Right over there, sir."

I raised my eyebrows at the clerk in commiseration. He looked past me again.

"Good morning, Mrs. Avery. How may I help you?"

"I think you need to help her first," rasped a voice. "She's been waiting."

A white-haired old lady had come up behind me. She was tiny, dressed in a red brocade Chinese jacket and flowing black trousers.

"Thanks." I shot her a smile. "Maggie Sullivan," I said to the clerk.

"Oh, yes. Mr. Tucker's expecting you." He gestured weakly. "In his office. I'll get your key."

Mrs. Avery chuckled.

"You okay, honey? It's a wonder Archie didn't knock you over. Damn fool thinks the world revolves around him." Her birdlike eyes took in my folded up ruler. "You some sort of decorator?"

"No, I'm—"

"Any book stores around here?" she asked the clerk as he returned. "I mean good ones, not some cigar stand with magazines and those flimsy paperback things."

I felt a presence at my elbow.

"Miss?"

The creased face of the bellman smiled up at me as he reached for my suitcase. His skin was weathered, as leathery as the luggage he moved. The pillbox strapped under his chin, coupled with a stature smaller than Wee Willie's and a bandy-legged gait, brought to mind the unfortunate image of an organ's grinder's monkey.

"I'm Smith, miss. I'll take this up to your room. Oh, no need for that." He tucked his free hand behind him as I tried to give him a tip. "Mr. Tucker already saw to it. Anything else you'd like me to do for you while you're here — anything — just ask."

A pair of bright eyes met mine as if to convey a message.

* * *

Without the suitcase, I was free to have my first real look at the lobby. The registration desk was to my left. Across the way a wide arch opened into the hotel lounge, which judging by its size was intended only for guests. At the rear of the lobby, centered, was the elevator. Beside it a carpeted staircase wound up to the floors above. Halls on either side of stairs and elevator led to rooms further back.

Resisting an urge to match my steps to the fleurs-de-lis pattern, I followed royal blue carpet toward the hall on the left and the door the desk clerk had indicated was Tucker's office. Just beyond, in the hallway itself, Archie Clarke was ensconced in a glass-doored phone booth. He appeared to be shouting.

"Sure glad to see you," Tucker said when he opened the door in response to my tap. Shadows under his eyes told of a night short on sleep.

"I hope things are going better than yesterday."

"They couldn't go much worse." He knocked on the edge of his desk and attempted a smile.

Like the man who occupied it, the office was small, but it was on the plush side, with a carpet and a drinks cabinet. Across from his desk, a big, gaudy, theatrical poster in a frame decorated the wall. The safe at the heart of his problems was also in the wall across from his desk.

Tucker waved me toward a chair and sank wearily into his.

"The police... well, they didn't exactly arrest me, but they took me downtown and kept asking me questions, some of 'em over and over. It shook me plenty, I tell you. They kept me till almost ten. Poor Frances was beside herself. She stepped right in and cracked the whip here, though.

"They were decent enough about it. The police. I'd asked could they please not bother the guests, and they didn't. Just stayed back in the housekeeping office and talked to the staff."

If the cops had held back, it told me they hadn't found anything concrete suggesting a link between victim and guests.

"They came to see me," I said. "Wanted to know what I was doing here."

"Oh, yeah. They asked me, too. I told them that about checking people we might hire."

"They seem to think you were having an affair with Polly."

41

His mouth opened wordlessly.

"I don't know whether to laugh or be insulted," he said at last. "I have NEVER cheated on Frances. Not once. Never even thought about it." There were tears in his eyes. "I love her!"

"I know you do. The problem is, you fired a man for making a pass at her. The cops think it shows more interest than a boss ordinarily takes in something like that."

His gaze faltered.

"So. You mind telling me why you didn't mention it to them? Because I'm guessing you didn't, which just about guaranteed they'd wonder why."

His bottom lip pushed out. That was as close as his face could come to the unfamiliar contours of anger.

"It wasn't none of their business."

"And the reason you didn't tell me? After hiring me to try and help you? After I specifically asked whether anyone had a grudge against you and might want to even scores?"

"It didn't seem important," he muttered.

"What didn't seem important?" Frances slid through the door. She had a mug with a saucer on top in her hand.

"Telling me he'd fired someone when I asked if anyone had a beef with either of you. He didn't tell the cops either."

"Kenny Stone, you mean? Oh, Joshua." The last two words came out in a sigh, as though she'd repeated them often.

"He couldn't have been the one getting into the safe." Tucker crossed his arms stubbornly. "He's not smart enough, and he'd never have nerve — for that or killing Polly either, if you're wondering. He's a sniveling jerk who couldn't keep his nose out of the sauce."

I shoved Tucker's desktop notepad toward him.

"I want his address." He opened his mouth to argue. "Or I'm done here."

"Oh, for God's sake, Joshua, do as she asks!" Frances set the mug at her husband's elbow. "And tell her the rest. No, I will. Kenny made a pass at me too — got me into a corner and tried to kiss me. That's why Joshua really fired him. He probably didn't tell the police — or you — out of some silly notion of - of protecting my honor."

"You've been through enough." Tucker slid Kenny Stone's address toward me. "I didn't want them grilling you. Wearing you out."

He was the one who looked worn out at the moment. He noticed the mug beside him.

"What's this?"

"Cocoa."

"Cocoa? It's not winter."

"You need something in you besides coffee. It will give you some energy."

The back of her hand stroked his cheek. I looked away with a pang. No one had ever touched me with such loving concern. Or maybe they had, and I'd pushed away.

NINE

While Tucker drank his cocoa, I asked if they still wanted to hide the truth about who I really was and why I was at The Canterbury. When they insisted they did, I told them the reason I planned to use instead.

"Motion engineering?"

The Tuckers stared at me blankly.

"It's another name for time and motion studies," I said. "Measuring how far workers have to move to perform a task, timing the parts that go into it, seeing what can be changed to increase productivity."

Frances understood first. "An efficiency expert!"

"Yes."

"It sounds ghastly dull."

"Meaning no one will want to hear much about it."

A woman named Lillian Gilbreth, along with her late husband, had pioneered the techniques. After his death she'd continued their work. When Purdue University named her a professor of engineering, stories about a woman being admitted into a man's field had popped up in papers and magazines. The public library hadn't had anything by the Gilbreths, but a friend had found a book by them down at the University. The few paragraphs I'd managed to make my way through gave me more than enough information to make people's eyes glaze.

"That's why you're toting that ruler," said Tucker. "So you can pretend to measure things and write on that clipboard. You'll be able to poke around everywhere, ask all kind of questions, and nobody gets the least bit suspicious."

For the first time that morning, he started to grin.

A knock interrupted. The Tuckers froze. Yesterday a similar knock had brought nothing but problems. Frances went to the door, opening it just wide enough to converse.

"We're in a meeting.... Ten minutes.... Oh, all right. I'll be there in two."

She came back to join us. There was a new steadiness about her today.

"It seems there are problems finding a substitute for Polly. I'll take care of it. Anything else here before I leave?"

"I need a list of all the current guests who were here on Wednesday and the whole week before that. Were any of them here as far back as when the man went missing?"

They looked at each other.

"I don't think.... Wait. The Szarenskis arrived somewhere near the end, didn't they?" Frances rubbed her forehead. "The day we called the police, I think. But not while the man was here."

"You're not saying a guest could have... could have...." Tucker struggled to grasp it.

"We need to look at all the possibilities," I said, and wondered if I sounded like Freeze.

* * *

When Frances left to tend to the crisis in housekeeping, Tucker opened the safe to give me a view of the cases inside. Mostly black velvet, as we'd discussed. He explained the hotel's procedure of assigning a number to each item put in the safe. He showed me the logbook where every movement in or out of the safe bore the item number, date and time, along with two signatures: that of the person who took or returned it, and Tucker's, or that of William, his manager.

"I thought you told me Frances knew the whole procedure as well."

"She does. At least, I had her do it a couple of times when we were first starting so she'd know how it worked, but she doesn't do anything involving the front desk. Her part's to oversee housekeeping, kitchen, the dining room. She does the ordering, picks the suppliers to use, keeps track of expenses. We divvy things up."

"When a guest first puts a case in, how do you know there's jewelry inside?"

His expression turned sheepish. "We look. Not in front of the owner, but first chance we get. Now and then a case has a lock, so all we can do then's shake it."

Sifting through what I'd gleaned about the safe's operation in hopes of finding something useful would take time. Meanwhile, being inside the hotel was like being dumped out in an unfamiliar neighborhood. I had to learn its streets and alleys.

"I need you to show me around," I said. "Make some introductions while I get a feel for the layout."

"Sure thing. There'll be more than a few people waiting to pounce on me the minute they see me anyway."

Taking a breath, Tucker drew himself up to what height he could muster.

"Okay, kid," he said with a wink. "Curtain going up."

* * *

For the next hour or so, I traipsed after Tucker. I met William, the manager, a reserved old gent with noticeable arthritis in his fingers. I met the desk clerk who'd ignored me earlier and now acted faintly embarrassed. I met the maître d' and the bartender who had replaced the one fired.

Every dozen steps, or so it seemed, someone on the staff stopped Tucker to ask or tell him something. He called each one of them by name. He introduced me as an efficiency expert, calling me "Miss Sullivan" or "Margaret". I asked random questions — what was the busiest hour for lunch; what was the average number of tables occupied — and scribbled pointless notes on my clipboard.

Whenever Tucker got tied up talking to someone, I unfolded my ruler and measured. I was jotting away after one performance when I felt someone watching. Glancing up, I tried not to stare. A man sat on the couch in the small conversation area. He looked as if half his face had been painted over, erasing his features.

"I guess I can't put off in back any longer," Tucker sighed.

His reluctance became clear as soon as we stepped through a swinging door into the kitchen and housekeeping department. At the sound of his voice a rail-thin woman with a silk chrysanthemum cringing on her bosom, flew out of a side room and lit into him. Miss G. It had to be. Her eyes gave me the Brillo pad treatment.

"Efficiency expert? I'll tell you how to be more efficient right now," she snapped. "Hire somebody to replace that silly girl who got herself killed."

Not exactly a font of compassion.

While the two of them argued about how to keep things sparkling until they found another girl to clean at night, I studied the kitchen that stretched almost the entire width of the hotel. The kitchen door stood open to the alley. Two men were lugging in bushels of apples. Polly Bunten's body had been discovered in a garbage can two buildings down.

A white-clad chef and his assistant barked orders as underlings jiggled past each other, chopping, stirring, and setting out platters. It wasn't their lunch preparations which held my attention, however. It was a staircase squeezed into one corner of the kitchen. Those stairs must be how chambermaids and room service waiters went up and down to the rooms above without bothering guests.

It also made a handy way for someone to slip up and down unseen. Especially in the dead of night.

TEN

Seeing how many demands were made on Tucker's time was an eye-opener. Assuring him I could find a room one floor up on my own, I picked up my key. Tucker handed me another of his cards. This one had a number written on the back.

"That's our private number. Nobody has it but William. It rings day or night."

There wasn't anything to notice inside an elevator. Besides, Tucker had told me it was locked every night at half-past twelve and out of operation until six the next morning. I climbed the stairs to the second floor. The room I was to occupy was immediately across from me, next to the elevator. As I fitted my key in the lock, I heard another door open softly. Before I could determine where it was, it clicked shut.

The room I let myself into was a far cry from Mrs. Z's, or anywhere else I'd ever spent the night. My feet left indentations in the thick carpet. Floating on one edge of it was a double bed with a padded headboard covered in cream colored satin. Embroidered garlands of pink flowers embellished the satin. A single small window looked out on the building next door. The window's pale green draperies matched the bedspread. A nightstand held a telephone and a lamp with a rose colored shade. I was glad no one had accompanied me, leaving me free to gawk.

The biggest luxury was the bathroom I'd have entirely to myself. At Mrs. Z's, a dozen of us shared. A tiled ledge surrounding the tub on three sides held soaps and bottles of bath oil.

Smith had left my suitcase on a folding luggage rack. I shook out my one-and-only other suit and opened the closet to hang it. Someone tapped on the door.

"Miss Sullivan? It's Frances Tucker."

She hugged a manila envelope to her chest as she entered.

"I thought I'd be formal in case anyone overheard," she said when the door had closed. "Smith told me he'd just seen you head up. I hope you don't mind the small room —"

"It's wonderful. Thanks."

"Here's a list of our employees, and one of who was here when the man went missing, and some other things you may find useful. She gestured toward a slipper chair. "May I?"

She pulled it up and perched on the edge. Taking several sheets of paper from the envelope, she spread them on the bed, pointing as she talked.

"I've made some rough floor plans so you can get an idea of rooms and where people are. This is your floor, for example. Count Szarenski and his family are here, in a suite that's far too small for four people, really. They've put their daughter in what's intended as the maid or valet's room, poor thing. Loren Avery and his mother are here, across from them."

The perky old lady in the Chinese get-up had been named Avery, I recalled.

"Next to the Averys we have Lena Shields, in our smallest suite," Frances was saying, "with her boyfriend — his name's Nick — conveniently next door in a room much like yours. They're the pair who were having the blowup yesterday."

She hesitated.

"Be wary of Nick. I overheard two women who stayed here last week gossiping about him. They'd seen him at some resort when he was with a different rich girl. They seemed to think he's a fortune hunter."

"That should eliminate me."

She laughed. "He might be a womanizer as well. And he can turn on the charm when he wants. I've seen him in action with some of the guests."

Legs tucked under me, I sat on the bed and watched as her finger moved over the rest of the drawings. The names of each room's current occupants had been written in. That was handy. I started to think Frances had a better grasp than her husband of what information might be useful to me.

"Who's Bartoz?" I asked, reading the name directly across from Lena Shields.

"He's with the Szarenskis. He's the count's, um, aide de camp, I guess you'd say. He was with the count in the army." Frances made a small face. "I'm afraid I don't really like him. He stands around and watches people."

"Anyone in particular?"

"No, I don't think so. And maybe he's not actually looking at anything. It may just seem that way because, well, he has only one eye. And he seems rather cold."

The man whose face had unnerved me, I thought. He must wear some sort of mask or flesh colored eye patch.

"Are some of the names on these floor plans people from Hollywood?"

"Yes, the Clarkes and Ronnie — Veronica Page — and a few others. I'm not sure what they're doing in Dayton. It's all quite hush-hush. Why?"

"I just seemed to recall your husband mentioning something about it the day he came to see me. I wanted to be prepared and not jump to conclusions if someone acts screwy."

She laughed again and checked her dainty gold wristwatch.

"I must get back downstairs and do what I can to help Joshua. Miss Gumm keeps going on about being one person short as if it's the only concern in the whole place."

* * *

The other pages from Frances' envelope helped me piece together the rest of the hotel's layout. The second floor, where I was, had more rooms than suites. On the floor above, there were slightly larger suites but only two rooms. The top floor had just four large suites, plus the double one the Tuckers occupied.

The rear of the hotel, where the count's suite and the Averys' suites were located, overlooked the alley. Those two suites were closest to the fire escape, which had a window opening out to it. They were also closest to the service stairs. Lena Shields and boyfriend Nick weren't much farther away, however. The metal fire escape stairs probably went all the way up to the Tuckers', but the back stairs used by the hotel staff must end on the floor above me and pick up in a new location to reach the top.

When I could, I'd take a stroll through the floors above me. For now, I looked at who was staying where. Except for Mrs. Avery, only two names were familiar. Archie Clarke, the guy who'd pushed in yelling about a telegram, was on the top floor. So was Veronica Page, the actress whose name had nearly caused Jenkins to turn cartwheels.

I put the floor plans back in their envelope and stowed them with a library book and my folding ruler. I didn't think that accessory for my little charade was necessary when I went down to lunch. The dining room, I figured, was the ideal place to get a look at some of the people staying here. Resisting the urge to try the inviting bed with its pile of pillows, lest I inadvertently close my eyes, I headed down.

The staircase to the lobby had the added advantage of giving a view of everyone milling about below. As I neared the bottom, I saw the old lady in the red Chinese jacket coming out of the lounge. Her arm was linked with that of a man half her age. His head bent solicitously as he talked. She brushed a hand at him in dismissal.

"Go hold Archie's hand," she told him as I turned toward the dining room. "You know I'll be fine on my own. We can knock around some other time."

Catching sight of me, the old woman came to a halt. Her gaze sharpened.

"You," she boomed, pointing at me with a finger whose nail was as red as her jacket. "Get over here."

ELEVEN

I drifted over, wondering what in the devil I'd done. I'd barely exchanged half a dozen words with the woman earlier.

"Go on now," the old lady said to the man beside her. "Butter our bread."

She offered her cheek, which he kissed obediently. It won him a pat on his arm. Thanks to Frances' briefing, I guessed he must be the other Avery, the son. As he turned away, Mrs. Avery planted her hands on her hips and gave me the once over.

"Tell me, girl-who's-not-a-decorator, are you from around here?"

"Not too far away."

"Are there any museums in this city worth seeing?"

"There's a really nice art museum."

It was new, ten years old. I went every chance I got.

"Does it have any nudes? I'm partial to nudes."

"Uh, probably. To tell you the truth, I've never noticed."

She chuckled, a hearty sound midway between laugh and cackle. Whether at my reply or because she was testing me, I couldn't guess. I also wasn't sure how Miss Efficiency Expert ought to react.

"Is it open today? Do you know? My son and I were going to see the sights in the area, but now he's got to pacify Archie Clarke and get him simmered down."

Clarke was the one who'd been in a tizzy over a telegram. I smelled opportunity.

53

"Oh, I know it's open," I said. "In fact I was going over myself after I checked one more thing here." I hesitated with what I hoped was the right amount of reticence. "I've got a car. I'd be glad to give you a lift."

"Honey, you've got a deal." Mrs. Avery broke into a grin. "You give me the ten-cent tour and lunch is on me."

* * *

I'd gambled on a few hours with Mrs. Avery yielding more information than sitting in the hotel dining room. It was a smart bet. She talked almost nonstop from the minute I helped her into my DeSoto. It wasn't mindless chatter; she was an intelligent woman, well read and interested in everything we passed.

She said we ought to eat before we hit the museum, so I took her to a two-story red building on Springfield Street. It was far enough out that no one who knew me was likely to come ambling up. The Union Stockyards once had occupied the spot.

"You're okay," Mrs. Avery said as we sipped gin and tonics. "Not nearly as dull as that job of yours makes you sound."

She'd made a face when I answered her question about why I had the ruler. She didn't seem eager to know any more when I told her I did time-motion studies.

"What about you?" I asked. "You said your son was here on some kind of business?"

"He's a choreographer. He's working on Archie Clarke's big new picture. There, that's all I'm allowed to say." She twisted a hand in front of her lips as if locking them.

I made a pretense of frowning.

"Clarke. That's the man who was upset over the telegram? Gee, I hope it wasn't telling him a relative died."

The old woman snorted. "Archie wouldn't put his fork down for that. His biggest star just wired from Havana saying she won't get here til Monday. Routes out of France were all blocked so she and the people she's with had to sneak into Greece and then hire somebody with a yacht to bring them to Cuba. We haven't heard from her in almost two weeks. Loren's been frantic."

It took some effort to absorb the reality of what she was saying. It took even more to maintain the role I was playing.

"It's that bad over there?"

Her head bobbed affirmation as she cut into the steak just placed before her.

"That's why Loren and I came back last fall. When Hitler went into Poland, it didn't take specs to read the handwriting on the wall. Those Nazis were likely to march into France; maybe even cross the channel. We didn't want to get stuck."

She popped a bite of meat into her mouth and gave a moan of pleasure as she chewed.

"Now this is what I call a steak."

It signaled her desire to change the subject, which was fine by me. An unseen shadow had edged its way onto our table.

* * *

Eulahbell's stamina put to shame that of women half her age. As we crossed the river and she got her first view of the tile roof the Art Institute on its hill, she exclaimed with delight. Inside, she set course immediately for the double staircase. Her red jacket bobbed in front of me as she raced up the marble steps.

We trotted through every floor and saw, I felt certain, every painting, plate and statue in the place. I managed to learn a couple of things about people at the hotel. Veronica Page was "a swell gal" who traded books and recommendations with her whenever they bumped into each other traveling. The actress coming from Cuba was named Mitzi, and she was "a ball of fire". While vacationing in France, she'd struck up a friendship with an American woman married to a Frenchman, and when he was killed and things fell apart faster than anyone anticipated, the two of them had thrown in together to get out of the country. Eulahbelle Avery traveled with her son because he wouldn't hear of her staying alone and she wasn't about to have what she considered a nursemaid.

When we finally returned to the hotel, I let her out at the door. Eulahbelle thanked me effusively. I parked in a gravel parking lot halfway down the block that had some spaces set aside for hotel guests and took my sweet time walking back. The small lounge at the hotel was deserted, which I took to be a sign I should slake my thirst and do a little more work before heading upstairs.

"What will it be for the lovely Miss Sullivan?" the bartender asked as he straightened from the afternoon paper spread on the bar before him.

My eyebrows raised.

"You know my name?"

"Yep. Got the word you're here doing efficiency studies. What's your poison?"

"Martini with an extra olive."

According to the list Frances had given me, his name was Len Welles. His brown hair was just unruly enough to be on the sassy side. He'd replaced the man who was fired, and Polly's death made him the hotel's most recent employee.

"On the house," he said, sliding the glass in front of me and crossing his arms on the bar with a grin.

"Oh, I couldn't," I said primly.

"Oh, you must. I'm wildly inefficient. I'm going to need personal tutoring to bring me up to snuff."

I laughed in spite of myself. He was flirting. The question was, what lay behind it?

Len was a bit too breezy for an establishment like The Canterbury. It made talking to him all the more fun. His fingers were smooth and well-tended enough for safe cracking, but that applied to quite a few men in the hotel. Trimming my list of suspects here wasn't going to be easy.

Halfway through my martini three men came in engaged in affable disagreement.

"Come on, if Congress agrees to send weapons to England and Germany defeats them, the Germans will turn around and use those weapons against us."

"And if we don't send them, England doesn't have weapons to defend itself!"

"Because they left their own tanks in France when they retreated."

Bypassing the bar, they went to a table.

"Engineers here to meet with Boss Kett. Got in this morning," Len whispered as he left to wait on them.

I used the opportunity to slip away.

A girl now occupied one of the chairs in the conversation area near the elevator. She was maybe fourteen with a round face and hair so brown it was almost black. It coiled in a braid at the crown of her head. She was looking down at her lap and chewing her nails with a vigor which made me wince.

I'd been a nail biter once, when I was younger than this girl. A woman my father knew had told me I had pretty hands and ought to wear nail polish. She'd held them in hers and filed and fussed, and then used pale pink polish which she gave me to keep. It was only later that I learned the truth about Maeve Murphy and my father.

On the couch to the right of the girl sat the man with the distorted face, the one I now knew to be Bartoz. He was facing the door, as if to keep tabs on everyone who entered the lobby. There was something insolent in the way he sat. Defiance over his missing eye? A black patch would have drawn little notice. The flesh-colored one he wore instead was jarring.

As I passed, I sensed more than heard him stand up behind me. I started up the stairs. At the second floor, I veered to the edge of the landing. I gripped the railing and peered down at the lobby. A few steps behind me, Bartoz also came to a stop.

When I glanced in his direction, his cheek bones darkened.

"Nice view from up here, isn't there?" I said cheerfully.

He sneered as he passed, and didn't answer. Maybe he didn't speak English. Maybe I didn't merit an answer from someone who worked for a count.

I turned and watched as he disappeared down the corridor toward his room. Then I took a final look down at the girl in the lobby. She'd given up chewing her nails. She was looking up now. When she realized I'd noticed her, she scowled.

TWELVE

I managed to survive my lack of popularity by taking a long bath and testing the bed. Then I drove to the Jenkinses' apartment where we drank and talked and ate while Jenkins waited in vain for an opening that would let him work conversation around to guests at The Canterbury.

"Oh, go ahead and put him out of his misery. He's been a good boy," Ione said when we'd adjourned to the living room.

Jenkins' wife was a good-looking ash blonde who caught your eye because of the intelligence crackling through her. She was on the couch with stocking feet tucked under her. Her hazel eyes shimmered with amusement.

"Good? He fidgeted all through dinner," I objected.

"Yes, but he didn't actually *ask*. I'd threatened him."

Jenkins, seated next to her, groaned.

"Come on, Mags. You promised. And don't think I'm not sore at that trick you pulled about the body they found in the alley."

"Oh, okay. But if you show your nose before I give you the go-ahead—"

"I won't."

"He won't." Ione nudged his thigh with her toes. "He doesn't like losing privileges."

"Okay. I already told you Veronica Page was there."

"Yeah. Who else?"

"A hotshot producer named Archie Clarke, along with his assistant and — are you ready for this? — a masseuse."

"Never heard of him." Jenkins was leaning forward with his elbows steepled on his knees. "Who else?"

"There's also an actress named…" I paused to get his saliva flowing. "Mitzi Cassingham."

Both of them grew excited. Because Jenkins lived and breathed pictures in any form, they went to the movies a lot more than I did. It appeared that while Mitzi hadn't gotten top billing in anything that they could remember, she was in plenty of films and becoming well known.

"She'll make a dandy story for you, too," I said. "Nearly got stuck in Europe and had to take a boat to Cuba."

Letting him think she'd already arrived ensured he wouldn't hang around the station when the train she was on was due.

"So when do I get to kick it into the newsroom? And take pictures?" he asked bluntly.

"A week or two." I waved off the start of his squawk. "Meanwhile, I might be able to give you something even better."

Jenkins was barely managing to stay on the edge of the couch now. Ione had switched her legs from one side to the other. She looked nearly as interested.

"Did you ever buy one of those home movie cameras like you were talking about?"

"Yep, a Baby Pathé. Cost me every bonus I've had this year and then some. Why?" He was getting suspicious.

"Has Ione ever used it?"

"Ione? I showed her a thing or two when I first got it — but I'm not showing you, and you're not borrowing it."

"You showed me more than a thing or two, you were so excited. And I might have tried it a time or two while you were at work," she said sweetly.

"Ione! Do you have any idea how much that film costs?" His voice went up half an octave.

"Oh, simmer down, Sparky. I only ran it for a minute or two."

"I don't want to use it. I don't want to touch it," I reassured.

I'd had an idea which might help me figure out what was going on with the hotel safe and keep Jenkins eating out of my hand at the same time. The next part was tricky, though.

"What I thought," I continued, "was that in exchange for keeping your nose out until I give the go-ahead, you might like to have a home movie or two."

It took several seconds. Then his words raced to his already opening mouth.

"You mean — inside the hotel? Of *them*? Mitzi? Veronica? You can pull that off?"

"*If* you do as I say. Or rather if Ione does. She'll be running the camera."

"Ione! Why not me? I'm the photographer."

"And they'd know within seconds that you were filming them. You'd be fiddling. Hunting a better angle. You wouldn't be able to help yourself. Ione can make it look like all she's interested in is how hotel employees do things. Like it's part of my time-motion studies."

Ione clapped her hands together.

"Oh boy! Ohboyohboyohboy!"

* * *

I returned to the hotel before eleven. The lobby was empty of guests. A kid who couldn't be dry behind the ears occupied the bellman's stand. The front desk looked unattended, but through the open door to the office behind it, I could see a night clerk. Since he was around all night, and his movements unlikely to draw attention, he'd be a prime candidate for checking.

As I passed the lounge, I saw Veronica Page and a few other people I didn't recognize laughing over drinks. The dining room was closed for the night. I eased open the door and peeked inside, but it was empty, and quiet as the moon.

Everywhere I walked, thick carpeting soaked up all sound from my steps. If a thief exercised a smidgen of caution, he'd be able to move about undetected. When I reached the swinging door to the kitchen, I leaned an ear close and listened. Nothing. I nudged it open an inch. A glimpse of a waiter disappearing up the service stairs with a tray rewarded me.

The vast space before me looked even larger empty of people and bustle. A couple of small lights were on, but the kitchen was full of shadows. The alley door was closed and presumably locked. I'd check from the outside tomorrow. Lots of people went out on a Saturday night, meaning streets and even alleys were busy. Sunday would be quieter, better for having a look at the rear of the hotel. Or for tinkering with a safe if someone meant to.

I let the door swing closed and, after a bit more prowling, headed upstairs. The second floor was quiet. So was the third floor. On the fourth, I caught the faint sound of a radio, or maybe a phonograph, from one of the suites. I went back down to my own room, fitted the key in the lock, and flipped on the light.

For several seconds after I'd closed the door, I stood frowning, trying to shake off the feeling someone had been there in my absence.

The pretty bed looked just as I'd left it. On the bedside table, the lamp with the rose colored shade seemed undisturbed. Folded up in the purse on my arm were the floor plans from Frances, the only evidence that might cast doubt on the role I was playing. Still, something didn't seem right.

Opening the closet, I examined my clothes. Just in case whoever was up to no good had gotten curious about me, I'd pulled one small corner in the lining of a suit pocket inside-out. Any intruder worth a fig would turn the pockets out to search them. When they put things to rights to cover their tracks, they'd inadvertently push the lining back into proper alignment. The corner was still out of place.

Only when I picked up the clipboard and pencil I'd left on the dresser was I sure I'd had a visitor. I sat down, uncertain whether to laugh or to be uneasy.

Someone had been in my room all right. They'd helped themselves to two sheets of paper where, while strolling around with my folding ruler, I'd written random measurements and occasional notes which were absolutely meaningless.

.

THIRTEEN

Sunday morning the sparsely populated dining room made me think most guests at The Canterbury must opt for breakfast in bed, at least on weekends. I read the paper and when I came to the page with the railroad timetable, thought of Connelly in Chicago. Was the girl he'd gone to meet someone he'd known back in Ireland? He spoke of his family often enough, but he'd never given any hint that he'd left a sweetheart behind. Was she pretty?

I couldn't bear to think about it anymore. I put the paper aside and finished some waffles with blueberries. Then I made a circuit through the ground floor to see how the hotel's rhythm varied today, and who on the staff was where. I noticed Tucker was in his office and rapped on the open door.

"Got a minute?"

"Sure." He capped his fountain pen and motioned for me to close the door behind me. "That was nice, what you did for Mrs. Avery yesterday, taking her somewhere."

"She's not bad company."

I told him about the papers missing from my room.

The little guy looked so miserable that I told him a woman I knew would pretend to take movies the following day to add to my time-motion studies charade. I might have given the impression there would be no film in the camera.

"Now I have a question," I said. "Frances gave me diagrams yesterday that showed who's staying in each of the rooms. Any idea why the Averys don't have a suite on the top floor like the other important movie people?"

His impish grin limped back where it belonged.

"Oh, sure. Lily — that's Archie Clarke's wife — doesn't like Eulahbelle. Lily wants people to recognize she's queen bee; bankrolls her husband's pictures, can nix somebody for a part if she gets it into her head. Eulahbelle doesn't kowtow. What Lily doesn't know is, Eulahbelle won't stay in a room higher than the second floor anyway. Got caught in a hotel fire when Loren was just a toddler."

The Averys' location probably wasn't important, but you never know.

"I've known some unpleasant people in my life," Tucker continued, "but Lily takes the cake. And talk about demanding!" He blew gustily. "She stayed behind in California for some charity bash. Arriving by plane this afternoon. I've put an extra room service man on just to take care of her."

I wasn't sure if he was kidding or not.

For the rest of the morning I crawled around and measured and listened at doors without hearing anything useful. I did satisfy myself that none of the maids could be a safecracker given the roughness of their hands from scrubbing toilets and changing linens.

Shortly before noon I drove to my office and took some scrunched up clothes from the bottom drawer of my file cabinet. It would be late when I stopped by for them that night, and I wanted to make sure I had everything I needed.

I thought better here, so I got out a tablet and pencil and noodled some. The people most likely to get into the hotel safe were those who were there at night. That narrowed it to employees who worked all night, or late, or came in early. And to guests.

Kenny Stone, the man Tucker had fired, had worked late. He probably nursed a grudge against both of the Tuckers. That made him a good place to start. Since Sunday afternoon was a nice time to pay social calls, I put on my hat.

* * *

"Kenny's not here," said the woman with ragged brown curls who answered the door where he lived. It was a two-story place halfway through being repainted. It sat on a street of modest homes with tidy yards.

"Oh, gee, I don't guess you'd know where I could find him?"

"Same place he always is when he lands in trouble, down at the church — for the third time today." Irritation oozed out of her as she looked me over. "If he owes you money, forget it. The idiot lost his job. If he got you in a family way, you're a worse fool than he is."

"Um no. Somebody left this lighter down at the bar Wednesday night. One of the men who works there said he thought it might be Kenny's. I was coming this way, so I offered to stop off and ask."

There's nothing like a thrift store lighter to help spin a tale. The woman sniffed.

"Kenny wasn't in any bars Wednesday. He was right here puking his guts out while I cleaned up after him. I just was getting him where he could keep down tea and crackers Friday when the cops came to talk to him, and there I go having to clean up again. Brother or not, he's out the door this week. With or without a job."

She slammed the door.

* * *

There wasn't anything else I could check on a Sunday, so I went back to the hotel. Smith, to my surprise, was in his bellman's spot.

"You don't get a day off?"

His leathery face smiled.

"I'm filling in so the other man can go to some family party. I'll get two days off next week or sometime I want 'em."

"Did Mr. Tucker tell you why I was here when he told you to help me out if I needed anything?"

He shook his head. His eyes were bright with curiosity.

"Doesn't matter. I'd still be swabbing decks on a ship somewhere if Mr. Tucker hadn't given me a chance to help with luggage in one of the shows he was with. I'd do anything he or the missus asked."

Nothing was going on in the lobby. It was a good time for talking.

"The man who disappeared a few weeks back, did you have any dealings with him? What can you tell me about him?"

Smith stood with hands clasped behind him, a navy pose that served him well as a bellman.

"One thing strange like" he said. "When he tipped me for taking his luggage up, he shook my hand."

"Most guests don't?"

"No, ma'am, but that's not the strange part. His fingers were callused. Hard callused. It could be 'cause he was one of those gents who dig up ruins in the desert or something like that, but he seemed... awkward, somehow. Like he wasn't sure he was doing things right."

"What did he look like?"

"Nothing special. Nothing to make you recall him. Brownish hair, I think, and average build. Roger might remember more. He's one of the waiters. Said the fellow ate like he was starving the first night he stayed here."

The desk clerk beckoned then, and Smith hurried off to find out where he was wanted. I made myself evident measuring and scribbling. Then I went to my room and sat on my bed with every fluffy pillow at my back and a book in my hand. Before I'd finished a single page, though, I found my thoughts drifting to Connelly again, and felt the wad of pain that had lodged inside me. I'd wanted him to abandon his determined pursuit of me, hadn't I? Or had I misinterpreted things he'd said? Deluded myself?

I shoved my thoughts back to the papers missing from my room.

What would possess someone to steal pointless scribbles? The obvious answer was that whoever took them didn't know they were pointless. Maybe they wanted the measurements I'd written. Only that made even less sense.

Finally I put on my blue winter dress and headed for dinner. Maybe I'd finally get a chance to study some of the guests. As I left my room and started toward the nearby elevator, a man turned away from it, spreading his arms to block me. It was Bartoz.

"Elevator not working?" I asked.

"Yes."

A thin red scar was visible above and below his eye patch.

"Gee, I thought I heard it coming up."

Behind him, the elevator clicked to a stop. The operator opened its polished brass grill to reveal an empty car. Bartoz seemed unfazed. Farther down the hall a door closed. A soft buzz of voices floated toward us, ceasing as I looked around.

A small entourage approached the elevator. Leading it was a thin man of medium height, his bearing so erect he might have swallowed a broom. Behind him, arm-in-arm, came two middle-aged women. Their clothes were expensive, and quietly stylish. One was dark and slender. The other was blonde and on the wrong side of plump. At the rear came the girl who had glowered at me in the lobby yesterday. A frown appeared to be her permanent expression.

I had no doubt at all that this was Count Szarenski and his family. I hadn't expected him to swagger around in a fancy uniform with a sash across it and a chest full of medals. Still, I'd hoped he'd at least wear the sash. To my disappointment he sported an ordinary tailor made suit.

Remote of manner, he took no notice of me as he walked past into the elevator. The others followed.

When they were all in, Bartoz stepped in too. He kept his back toward them. His arms remained spread.

"Sorry, it appears there's no room left," he said, startling me with his smooth British enunciation.

As the grill closed them in, his single eye met mine in challenge.

FOURTEEN

Being an American girl who understood democracy and sharing, I took the stairs. When I reached the short hall to the dining room, Bartoz lounged against the wall smoking. Did he serve as some kind of bodyguard, suitable to protect the count and his family, but not to join them for meals? I gave him a perky wave as I passed.

A waiter had scarcely pulled out my chair when Eulahbelle hustled over.

"It's no fun eating alone, honey. Come join Loren and me."

She was too good an information source to offend. It soon became apparent, though, that her purpose wasn't only hospitality, but matchmaking.

"Has her own car, knows how to entertain herself — you don't find many girls like that," she bragged when her son thanked me for taking her to the museum.

The choreographer looked uncomfortable. He was lean, with a startling amount of muscle. His face was too long to be handsome, but lines at his eyes and mouth suggested humor.

"You have a boyfriend?" Eulahbelle asked with unvarnished directness.

Her son sent me an apologetic look.

"Uh, yes," I lied as emptiness filled me.

Time for me to take control.

"I know you can't tell me anything about the picture you're working on, but I sure hope Miss Shields and that fellow she's with aren't supposed to be the lovebirds in it." I nodded toward Lena and Nick at a cozy table for two. "They had such a row in the lobby Friday, I thought they were going to hit each other."

Loren Avery snorted softly. His mother gave her distinctive chuckle.

"Neither of them has anything to do with Archie's picture. Acting, either."

"Oh. I just thought since they were staying here too, and everyone seemed to know them...."

"From over there." Eulahbelle waved vaguely, indicating Europe, I assumed.

"Americans abroad — theater people and writers and such at least — tend to wind up at the same parties," Loren clarified. "They stay at the same hotel sometimes, or cross on the same ship. I have to admit I couldn't believe it when Nick and Lena showed up here the day after we did."

"Like two bad pennies," Eulahbell muttered.

"Now, Mother. If it hadn't been for Nick, we wouldn't have found out about—" Looking sheepish, he tried to cover his near flub. "We wouldn't have found out what a nice place this is for rehearsing."

Why had Eulahbelle used the term 'bad pennies'? Right now, I wanted to nudge her son some more while he was off balance.

"Gee, I didn't think you had to rehearse a lot for a movie like you do a play," I said innocently.

"Uh, no. Not usually. But this one has some dancing—"

"*Lots* of dancing."

"Mother." It was the first time he'd spoken sharply. "One of the actresses has never danced, and another hasn't for a long time. That's why we're here. So... I can work with them."

His gaze slipped with the lie, and Bingo, I knew exactly why they were in Dayton: the Schwarz sisters. Hermene and Josephine Schwarz had become quite famous for their ballet school. They'd studied in Chicago, and one of them had performed in New York and Europe. The actresses were here for private coaching.

"Nick visits some elderly relative here," Loren was saying. "Grandmother or aunt. He overheard Archie trying to recruit me in our hotel in London and came around later to say he knew a spot that had what we needed. Easy to get to but not someplace where we'd have to duck photographers, and even with a good rehearsal space.... Look, please don't mention any of this."

I crossed my heart. The part about the movie wasn't important. Nick's hand in getting them here was interesting though.

"Well. I just hope he and his girlfriend don't have many fights like that one the other day," I said. "When I was unlocking my door this morning, I saw the two of them coming out of their rooms—"

"You're on our floor?" Eulahbelle winked reassurance. "It's quiet as can be. If some fool didn't keep opening the window and waking me up with the cold—"

"Mother, nobody opens the hall window."

"I saw it with my own eyes."

"When?"

"Last time I told you about it."

"You'd taken two of those pills for your back. They knock you out."

"They did — until I woke up shivering." She glanced over, enlisting my belief in her claim. "I went out to close it, and there was that man of the count's leaning out with his arms on the sill and a cigarette dangling out of his mouth. I asked could he please close the window and he nodded and went back to smoking. I don't think he understands English."

His English was excellent. I'd heard it. I wondered what night she was talking about.

"If they're not actors, what do they do?" I asked. "Miss Shields and Mr. — "

"Perry. Nick Perry." Loren sounded relieved at the change of subject. "I think Lena inherited money."

"Not a lot though. Her old man lost in the Crash. Some of what she lives on comes from writing filthy novels."

"Mother!"

"Well, it's true, honey. Published in Europe but banned over here. I tried one. You know some of the stuff I've read, but tying each other up and three in a bed? No thanks."

Conversation through the rest of the meal was light and enjoyable. From time to time I observed Nick and Lena, who showed no inclination to lean toward each other or touch like two people attracted to each other. I also took note of the count and his family. They sat together like strangers, him ramrod straight, the two women looking nervous and ill at ease. The girl chewed her nails.

Our waiter had just served meringues filled with ice cream and strawberries when a trickle of muted sound through the room announced the arrival of someone important. Looking up I saw Archie Clarke wending his way past tables. On his arm was a nondescript woman enhanced by money. Her chestnut hair swept to one side. Her dress with its narrow two-tier skirt and shoulder capelet, screamed Paris designer. Even with those touches, her only average face and figure might not have won a second look save for the pear shaped diamonds glittering at her ears and neck.

"Wow, those are sure some sparklers," I said. My whole body flinched at the thought of them in the hotel safe.

I watched in fascination as the Clarkes settled in at their table and people began to pay homage. A pair of young men hurried over to chat.

"That's Dan and Dave. They dance with the girls," whispered Eulahbelle.

One of the young men bent toward Lily Clarke's hand as if he meant to kiss it. Lily was lapping it up. Veronica sauntered over and said a few words. Even Lena Shields went to greet her, and appeared to be in full charm mode. Maybe, since she was a writer, she hoped to hitch her star to the Hollywood crowd.

My sense of uneasiness over Lily's jewels, and Tucker's safe, sharpened.

FIFTEEN

After nine o'clock, the damp-behind-the-ears night bellman doubled as doorman, standing just inside the entrance where he could handle both responsibilities. I winked as I went out. He blushed.

A skim of fog had moved in from the river. I drove to my office, glad to be prowling streets where I felt more at home than I did in The Canterbury. Luxury isn't everything.

The building was quiet. Sophia and Gilead, the Negro women who cleaned, didn't come in on weekends. Somewhere downstairs in a back room, there was a night watchman who came to life about as often as the spittoon in the lobby. Maybe he was related to the building manager.

In my office I switched on the desk lamp and changed into the clothes I'd put out that afternoon. My evening attire wasn't quite in the class of Lily Clarke's. Mine was men's trousers from the thrift store, a sturdy shirt, and a workman's jacket. Since I didn't have diamonds, I jazzed it up with a Smith & Wesson under my jacket.

It was still too early to head out, so I sat enjoying the familiar surroundings and thinking.

Mostly I thought about Lily Clarke's jewels.

There was no reason to think they'd be a particular target, what with a count's wife — I guessed that made her a countess — and a couple of actresses on the guest rolls. Still, they'd be hard to resist.

I poured myself some gin, but sipping it didn't seem to make me any smarter. At midnight I turned off the light and locked my door. Then I went to the alley where Polly Bunten had died.

* * *

I parked on the side street nearest The Canterbury's back door. For the first quarter hour I sat in the cozy confines of my DeSoto and studied the side windows of the hotel.

They looked out on a cross street and the ground floor sills were a good eight feet above the sidewalk. A very tall man might be able to reach them with his fingertips, but he wouldn't be able to pull himself up. As to getting out of the building, any intruder who tried to leave Tucker's office by way of the window risked breaking an ankle. A thief could drop something from the safe out the window, wait for the coast to be clear inside, then slip out and retrieve it. A spindly hedge between the hotel wall and the sidewalk might provide a small amount of cover for a bundle waiting to be retrieved, but just enough traffic passed, on foot and by car, to make that tactic risky.

The rear of the hotel seemed a more logical way for a thief to get in and out. Or for an employee to pass something to a confederate.

Crossing the street, I stood at the mouth of the alley, just out of sight. I waited and listened. After ten minutes, I'd seen no hint of movement and heard no sound save for an occasional car in the street behind me.

I stepped into the alley. Gliding over, I tested the kitchen door to the hotel. It was locked. A weak glow trickled out from the single light left on at night. All windows on the floors above were dark.

My eyes picked out a doorway suited to my purposes. With my back against the threshold and my knees drawn up, I made myself as comfortable as I could. I turned up my collar and snugged down the tweed cap hiding my hair. I pulled out the pint of gin that would make me look like dozens of other men sleeping one off. I took a swig to warm me. Then I waited.

Nothing happened.

A pudgy man shambled his way down the alley, looking in trash cans and muttering to himself. He didn't notice me. Around two a.m. I nodded off. All at once I came fully awake, aware of a sound.

My eyes were well adjusted to the dark around me. As they swept the area, I spotted a figure climbing stealthily up the fire escape. A man. Headed for a second story window, which now was open.

Silent as the bricks behind me, I slid to my feet. Several hours on the ground had stiffened my muscles. I flexed them as my hand crept toward my .38.

A quick glance around me showed only emptiness. I moved, darting across the alley. My foot found the first rung of the metal fire escape. I started up, eyes fixed on the figure above me.

Something whispered over my head. A metal wire circled my neck. Before I could react it bit in, jerking me backward.

SIXTEEN

Instinct to fight the tightening wire which would kill me in seconds drove out all other thoughts. I let the .38 fall from my grasp and grabbed with both hands for the wire.

Then I realized fighting the wire was exactly what my attacker expected. What he didn't expect was for me to grip his forearms as if they were bars and jerk my knees to my chest, curling toward the very weapon meant to end my life.

If he'd been larger he might have maintained his balance. Instead, my unanticipated weight pitched us both forward. We slammed into the metal stairs.

It caused my assailant to lose his grip on one end of the garrote. I flung myself to the side, rolling over the edge of the bottom few steps of the fire escape. The short fall onto the brick alley hammered my bones but I was free.

My fingers groped frantically at the ground beside the fire escape. They brushed what I was hunting. My Smith & Wesson. As soon as I found the trigger I fired, without caring where.

A snarl of rage rewarded me.

I fired again. I had no sense of where my attacker was. A voice hissed above me. Muffled steps ran. A window slid swiftly down.

Heart beating so I thought my chest would split, I pulled myself up. I gasped for air, coughed, tried again, felt it wheeze through my windpipe. When I put my hand to my throat, it came away wet.

"Everything okay?" The kitchen door of the hotel opened. A man who must be the room service waiter stood peering out.

"Car backfired," I rasped. I got to my feet. "Scared the bejeezus out of me. Even dropped my bottle."

The door clicked closed.

Breathing still didn't come easily. At the moment, I was glad it came at all. When I'd steadied some, I crossed the street and climbed into my DeSoto. I placed the Smith & Wesson on the seat beside me. I tilted the mirror to look at my neck. A narrow two-inch line across my windpipe bled merrily.

* * *

Running into the hotel the way I was dressed, with a bleeding neck, would cause too many questions. I drove to the office and dialed the nighttime number Tucker had given me.

"Check the safe," I said when he answered. "And check things on the second floor. Let me in the kitchen door in fifteen minutes."

He didn't waste time on questions. I hung up and sat at my desk with all the lights on. I'd never had a run-in with a garrote before, but I knew if my reactions had been a few seconds slower it would have strangled me, possibly cutting an artery on the side of my neck or crushing my larynx for good measure.

Whoever had gone in the window was playing for high stakes.

And he — or she — had an accomplice.

* * *

"The way you were attacked... it was the same as Polly, wasn't it?"

Frances bent over the back of the couch in their apartment winding a ribbon of gauze around my neck. I'd just filled them in on what occurred in the alley.

"Different method of choking." I wasn't sure about that, but her fussing embarrassed me.

"You're sure you don't want a doctor to look at this?"

"Thanks, but I'm okay."

As she tied off the gauze, I reached for the coffee cup sitting in front of me. On the opposite side of a low table Joshua Tucker was sipping whiskey, but I needed something to keep me awake. It was almost four in the morning.

"What about the safe?" I asked.

Tucker rubbed his hands together, faintly pleased.

"Didn't look to me like it had been touched. I used to manage a first-rate magician. It hit me yesterday I could use a trick of his to keep track of the boxes."

Tugging at the sash of her silky green dressing gown, Frances came around to settle on the couch beside me.

"This tonight, someone sneaking in a window, it proves Joshua was right about that empty box doesn't it? Somebody was — is — getting into the safe."

I nodded. The joe wasn't doing much to revive me.

"Why not grab everything at once? Why go in again?" Tucker rubbed his overnight stubble.

"Maybe the first time was testing the waters. Maybe they meant to make their real play tonight, but stumbling into me, and then you hotfooting it downstairs scared them off."

Maybe. Maybe, maybe.

Or maybe not.

"The smartest thing for you to do is hire a guard to sit in your office," I said. "Somebody in plain clothes."

"No."

"I can take what's left of tonight—"

"No."

"Just until I find out if there's some sort of burglar alarm you can get installed."

The stubborn little hotel owner was shaking his head.

"Too much hustle and bustle. It'd scare off whoever's doing this."

"Which is probably the smartest idea. I have to tell you, the chances I'll be around at exactly the right time to stop whoever wants in the safe, or figure out who that is beforehand, aren't good. And Archie Clarke's wife came into the dining room while I was there tonight. The diamonds she had on would choke an elephant."

Tucker's grin lacked its usual wattage, but it was there.

"I got confidence in you, kid. And I'm a good judge of talent."

"Besides, if we've got a rotten apple working for us, we want to know who," Frances chimed in.

It was just enough to keep him going when he might have seen reason. I tried a different angle.

"Do you know any jewelers who do appraisals? Ones you've dealt with and trust?"

"Sure," said Tucker. "We took some of Franny's jewelry to one a year or two back. Daniel-something. Nice fellow."

"Call him first thing tomorrow. This morning. See if he'll come have a look at what's in the safe and estimate what you'd be out if you lost the whole lot."

Hearing the price tag might scare some sense into them.

SEVENTEEN

Four hours of sleep and a bath revived me. At nine on the dot Ione strode into the hotel lobby and my jaw dropped.

Ione was wearing trousers. The soft, fawn colored flannel had been cut unmistakably for a woman's shape. The jacket matched. Her blonde hair was done up in a businesslike twist. With the poise of a general she marched toward me toting a square black case, which I could tell by the way she gripped it was heavy.

"Wow," I said. In a lobby accustomed to well-heeled clients with interesting trappings, several sets of eyes had nonetheless turned to take her in.

"One of my New York outfits," she said serenely. "I thought it might be appropriate."

Ione was building up nice success as a magazine writer. Once or twice a year she took the train to New York and met with editors who bought her pieces. Jenkins groused that she spent most of what she earned on clothes, but he was proud of her.

"Those two old biddies checking out look as if you've caused them to need smelling salts," I said.

"They'd better have a ton of it. Lots of women are wearing trousers. Is there some place I may set this? It weights a ton."

The desk clerk showed us a storage closet in the office area behind the desk. There Ione removed Jenkin's expensive toy from its case with appropriate care. All seriousness now, she went over it, making sure everything worked, and possibly reminding herself how it worked as well.

"Now," she said. "Have I instructions?"

"Right here." I waved my handy-dandy clipboard. "I'll point out areas and you'll take pictures with that wherever you like."

"Matching it at least somewhat to where you indicate."

"That would be nice."

Ione cocked her head.

"You look very nice with a scarf at your neck. I don't think I've seen you wear one before."

"Thanks."

Frances had pressed a couple into my hand as I left last night. The soft blue one I wore wrapped around my neck did a nice job of hiding the cut. It was scabbing over already, but still needed gauze here and there, and certainly camouflage. I didn't much like scarves, since one had nearly cost me my life, so it cheered me that someone with Ione's fashion sense liked the result.

We started our spot of play-acting in the dining room. I hadn't expected to see so many of the Hollywood people up and about. Archie Clarke sat with a younger man I didn't recognize. The two male dancers Eulahbelle had pointed out last night were there. So were the Averys, and Veronica. Added to the hotel guests who came and went, it made for the busiest breakfast setting I'd seen.

"Now follow that waiter when he starts back," I extemporized. I took out a stopwatch.

Ione spread her feet for steadiness and hefted the camera. I heard a faint whirling which I guessed was the key-wind mechanism Jenkins had chattered about.

We did the scene a few more times. Mostly I didn't hear any whirling. I clicked the stopwatch and jotted nonsense on my clipboard. I was pretty sure Ione had spotted Veronica Page by now, though she didn't let on.

"That line of navigation is particularly problematic." I waved toward a wall some distance beyond the actress.

Ione fiddled with some settings on the Pathé, then turned and started the camera running again. Veronica, who was reading the morning paper with a cup of coffee in one hand, didn't look up. Archie Clarke surged out of his seat like an enraged bull.

"Hey! Gimme that!" He grabbed for the camera.

Ione stepped back (still filming, I suspected) and swung a trousered leg around to block him. Veronica raised her head to see what was causing the ruckus.

"Don't you *dare* lay so much as a pinkie on my camera." Ione drew herself up and gave a fine appearance of glaring down at the chubby producer even though she was only an eyebrow taller. "Do you have any idea how much equipment like this costs?"

"Do I—?" Clarke sputtered. "Do you know who I am?"

"I don't care who you are, pal, keep your pudgy fingers away from this camera or you'll be hunting a dentist."

Clarke turned red enough to keel over. His younger companion hovered uselessly behind him. With a majestic flounce, Ione went back to filming.

Before the Hollywood bigwig could react to this added indignity, I took his arm and urged him away.

"She's awfully volatile," I whispered. "Gave another man who got in her way a huge black eye. But she's terribly good and we'll be finished here in a jiffy — just as soon as we have enough footage to analyze breakfast service."

"It's, uh, some sort of efficiency study for the hotel," the younger man said.

Clarke shook off my arm. Spewing angrily to his companion, he stomped back to his table. Veronica Page held a napkin to her mouth to cover laughter.

* * *

Ione and I took our little show to the kitchen. She pretended to film. I scribbled. The chef shot us uneasy looks. His assistant mugged. Just to provoke Miss G, I had Ione poke her camera into the housekeeping office. We emerged from the back hall into the lobby as Tucker and a pleasant looking man in a tweed jacket disappeared into Tucker's office.

"If you can spare the film, I'd like you to stand by this door and move it along to show everything you could see with your eye," I said in a low voice.

"The gangster checking to see if the coast is clear before he makes a run for it."

"Yes, like that. Then you can stop and we'll go across to the lounge. I want you to do the same thing over there."

I had no idea how long it would take to get the sort of film she was using developed. I didn't know if it would show anything I couldn't see with my own two eyes. What I was fairly sure of, based on my rambles through the hotel, was that one far end of the lounge was the only point in the lobby invisible to someone entering Tucker's office.

"Since we're right here, is it too early for a drink?" Ione asked when she'd finished the second part of her assignment.

"Not if we have Bloody Marys."

"Why don't you find a table and rest your tootsies," I said. "I want to powder my nose."

Mostly I wanted to see whether anyone was limping this morning, though I had no idea whether my wild shot last night had hit my assailant.

My fingers touched the scarf at my throat. Only a small cut; not stitches or broken bones, I reminded myself.

In contrast to the surprisingly busy dining room I'd encountered earlier, the lobby area now seemed emptier than usual. Veronica Page sat in the conversation area. She was juggling a book on her lap more than reading it. She checked a platinum wrist watch and glanced toward the lobby entrance. As she did, she spotted me.

"Tell your friend I could fill that dining room with people who'd pay ten bucks a head to see the performance she put on with Archie Clarke."

"Oh dear. One of the waiters said he's some sort of movie producer. Is he? We didn't know."

She shrugged.

"Don't worry about it. So you're doing some sort of efficiency study?"

"Yes, and we'll try not to bother—"

"You've got a job to do."

Her eyes went to the door again. She returned to her book. Interview over.

Continuing past her I reached the hall outside the dining room. A neatly groomed woman in a navy dress hovered there, peering into the lobby.

She wasn't quite gussied up enough to be a guest, but I hadn't seen her around before. I wondered who she was.

No one appeared to be limping. Ione and I had our perked up tomato juice and chatted about inconsequential things. We sauntered out of the lounge, with Ione capturing — or at least pretending to — a final sweep of the lobby before heading back to pack up her camera. In the midst of it the lobby door opened on such a commotion that every eye in the place turned toward a party of four.

Striding ahead of the others, determination in every movement, came a black-haired woman in a plain hat and dowdy dress. A woman, a boy of about nine and a sturdy older woman who looked like a servant trailed in her wake.

"If I never wear a wig again it will be too soon!"

Aware every eye was on her, the woman in the lead stripped off her hairpiece and sent it sailing across the lobby. She leaned on the counter and sent the desk clerk a smile that lighted the whole place.

"Ring Archie Clarke's room and tell him his lost lamb has arrived."

EIGHTEEN

The lobby exploded. Veronica sprang to her feet. Loren Avery appeared from nowhere muttering a fervent "Thank God!" With a cry of joy, someone shot past me. It was the plainly clothed woman who'd been peering out from the hall.

"Oh, this will be a much better study in luggage conveyance," said Ione innocently. Filming. Her subject appeared to be the items being carried in by Smith and another bellman, but I knew it was the newcomer, who without a doubt was Mitzi Cassingham.

To describe the actress as blonde was an understatement. Her newly freed hair was a cloud of spun sugar around an oval face. She spread her arms wide for the woman in the navy dress who hurtled into them.

"Oh, Miss! I've been so afraid for you!"

"I know you have, Till, and I'm sorry I put you through it. I had no idea I'd get stuck. Is your room okay? Are you okay?"

Something caught my eye on the balcony. Bartoz. Surveying the activity.

"You'll be doing a lot of shopping for me these next few days," Mitzi was telling her maid. "I barely have a change of clothes. For now, can you unpack my suitcase? And draw me a lovely, lovely bath."

As the maid hurried off, Veronica stepped close to drape an arm around Mitzi's shoulder.

"Late because you couldn't tear yourself away from cavorting with all those Greek sailors? That's how I heard it."

"Something like that." Mitzi laughed and nudged her with an elbow. "Good to see you, kid."

"Likewise."

Mitzi shook Loren's hand and apologized for delaying things. He said he was glad she was safe.

Ione lowered her camera.

"Have we gotten everything on your list?" she asked for any listeners.

I clicked the stopwatch off, then flipped some pages on my clipboard. I nodded. The elevator disgorged a stern looking Archie Clarke.

"Why don't you pack up? I want to make a few notes here while things are still fresh in my mind," I said.

Bartoz had vanished, but Lena Shields had appeared. She sat on one arm of the couch vacated by Veronica. Her gaze, however, wasn't on Mitzi. Hard to tell whether it was on the trio that had arrived with Mitzi or on the luggage behind them.

Mitzi's maid had shepherded Smith up with her single suitcase. What remained belonged to the threesome who'd come in with Mitzi. Three ordinary suitcases. Another one, child sized. And four very sturdy unfinished wooden crates. Two were nearly the height of the front desk. The others looked about as high as where my garter belt clipped to my stockings. Their width varied, but none of the crates was more than ten inches deep.

The owners of the luggage moved without animation, as if dazed or exhausted or both. The younger of the women was signing the register. She gripped the little boy with a ferocity that warned against trying to separate them.

Eulahbelle and the two male dancers ran up to join the throng around Mitzi. Archie Clarke was booming away. To my surprise, I saw Count Szarenski and his bunch making their way toward the new arrivals.

Their destination, however, wasn't the actress. As those with him halted a few paces back, the aloof Szarenski spoke to the woman clutching the little boy. She turned from the desk. Stopping in front of her, the count clicked his heels together, took her hand, and bowed low to kiss it.

As dazed as she seemed, the woman gave a small bow in return. They exchanged a few words in French, or maybe Polish, with him doing most of the talking. She took a lace-trimmed hanky from her pocket and dabbed at her eyes. One of the Szarenski women stepped forward and murmured something and bussed her on both cheeks. Meanwhile, the count leaned low on his cane to speak to the little boy.

Had he used a cane before? When they excluded me from the elevator?

I looked up to find Bartoz's single eye looking at me.

* * *

"Matt's going to be too excited to sleep."

"As long as he's too excited to renege on our deal."

Ione and I were on our way to the parking lot, but my mind was still on the scene in the lobby. The quieter one. The woman must be the young widow Tucker had told me about the day he hired me, the one whose husband had died fighting with the French resistance. Apparently he'd been well enough known, or his widow was, for a count from another country to pay respects.

"Can he have that film ready to watch tomorrow?" I asked Ione.

"Oh, I doubt it. This morning he said something about it having to go to Cincinnati."

"Cincinnati!"

She looked at me shrewdly.

"I'll tell him you need to see it pronto for whatever you're working on."

"Thanks, Ione."

"Which I now speculate has to do with those crated up paintings."

So that was what the crates contained. I'd supposed they held clothes. Since Ione moved in the sort of circles to know about such things, I decided she was probably right. I smiled noncommittally.

When we'd said our good-byes, as I started back in, I noticed the scowling Szarenski girl. She sat on the hood of a car parked under a spindly tree that was managing to hold its own in a far corner of the parking lot. As she caught sight of me, her expression grew almost civil. Then a voice spoke behind me and I realized she'd been looking over my shoulder.

It was Bartoz, and the words that passed between them were incomprehensible. Moving toward her, he spoke again, this time with a jerk of the head. I didn't need a translator to tell me it meant, roughly, 'Get inside and don't wander off again.'

The girl slid reluctantly from the car. For half a second I felt sorry for her. If her father was a count, the kid had probably had the run of a big yard with plenty of trees and things to do. Now she was stuck in a strange place with adults afraid to let her out of their sight.

I walked back to the hotel to find out what the jewelry appraiser had discovered. And how long Count Szarenski had been using a cane.

NINETEEN

The appraiser, a man named Daniel Drew, was just completing his work when Tucker opened the door a crack in response to my knock. He gestured me wordlessly into his office. One look at his face told me the news wasn't good.

"He's written it all up. See for yourself."

Sinking into his chair, the hotel owner pushed two sheets of paper across his desk. I'd managed to skim just a few lines before he summarized.

"Half the things in there are phony."

I looked up. Tucker's round face, which seemed designed for buoyant optimism, was drawn with despair.

Drew, in the midst of tucking an eye loupe into his pocket, glanced up.

"No more than a third of them," he said gently. "If that."

"Either way, we're still ruined—"

I held up my hand. Something was wrong. But possibly not what my client thought.

"First of all, has everyone with things in the safe been here for the past ten days?"

Tucker took the list back and hunched over it.

"Well, no...."

"Tell me, Mr. Drew, would it be unusual for a safe in a hotel like this one to have this many, uh, reproductions? In nice cases like the real thing?" I was on thin ice, but I didn't see how so many pieces could have been switched in such a short space of time.

Tucker squirmed. He most likely hadn't told the appraiser why he needed his services, or why with such immediacy. I figured Drew was smart enough to have guessed.

"Probably not." Drew hesitated, couching his words in caution. "I've never been asked to inspect the entire contents of a safe before, other than for private estates. I can assure you it's not uncommon for people who own expensive jewelry to have a very good copy made and seldom, if ever, wear the original. That would be particularly true when they traveled.

"And of course since the Crash, more than a few have sold a piece here or there to make ends meet, so to speak." His mouth gave a wry twist. "As to nice velvet cases, they're not that expensive. Cheap paste jewelry to use on stage is one thing, but a quality copy involves workmanship — not to mention the gold in the setting. You don't want something like that scuffing around."

I'd retrieved the list while he talked. A question mark by an entry on the second page caught my eye. Reading the name beside it, I did a double take.

"Why this question mark?" I pointed.

"Ah, yes." He didn't need to look. "I flatter myself that I have a very good eye, but that piece, a very old ruby necklace, I couldn't be entirely certain about the three main stones. There's a man in town who's a master copier, and so skilled at spotting such work that he often knows where it was made. Sometimes even by whom. I've suggested Mr. Tucker ask his opinion on this one."

When the dispirited Tucker walked him out a few minutes later, I finally had a good look at the list. Twenty-four jewelry cases, six of them containing fakes and one requiring a second appraisal.

One of the fakes, as well as the one with a question mark by it, belonged to the women with Count Szarenski.

Another belonged to Lena Shields. Three belonged to a name I didn't recognize; one to a likewise unknown guest. And there amidst the others snuggled Lily Clarke's four jewelry cases. Every sparkle inside them was genuine, beckoning a would-be thief like a virgin in a burlesque show.

Tucker returned and slumped in his chair.

"Insurance would cover two of those pieces, maybe three," he said after a minute. "But like I told you in the beginning, once word got out, we'd be ruined. And with so many phony, if something's happened to them while they were in our safe—"

"Slow down."

"If we had to make good on all of them.... The thing is, four months ago, when it was time to re-up the insurance, I reduced the amount. Frances... there were a lot of medical bills."

He looked at me in appeal. He didn't want her to know.

"You'll still get paid," he added quickly. "Everybody who works for us will. Don't worry none there."

"I wasn't."

"Now you gotta find out who's behind this. Those other things you suggested — a guard or alarm — it's too late for those, but if somebody's stealing, maybe we could still get things back, track them down."

"Joshua, I'm not going to tell you not to worry, but maybe you should worry less. Mr. Drew just told you owners themselves often get copies made."

His bullheaded insistence on secrecy whittled down chances I could do what he wanted, or even prevent further losses, but I had to try. He was my client. So long as it wasn't illegal, I did what a client wanted. Besides, somewhere along the line I'd started to like the little guy in his loud suits.

"Did Drew give you the name of that jeweler who's an expert on copies?" I asked.

"Lagarde." He took a slip of paper from his pocket. "Philip Lagarde. Has a place on First Street."

He handed me the note so I could write down the particulars.

"Let me have a talk with him. See what I can learn about how long it takes to make something like that."

When I got within a block of the address, however, I knew I wouldn't be chatting with anyone there in the next few hours. Parked in front were two police cruisers and an unmarked car that belonged to the homicide boys.

TWENTY

The location of Lagarde Jewelry, more than its bright blue awning, told me it catered to the carriage trade. It was in easy walking distance of the Hotel Miami and Rike's Department Store. Four years of working at the latter place before I set up shop as a gumshoe meant I had an ace or two up my sleeve.

I found a parking place, steering clear of the new meters on Main and Ludlow that had caused such a tizzy. Then I went into Rike's and caught up with Abner Simms, head of security. He immediately whisked me to lunch.

"Sure you won't come back to work for me?" Ab raised bristling brows and gave a tiny smile. "No getting punched in the nose, no sitting in the cold playing Peeping Tom, fancy sandwiches whenever you wanted them."

We were in one of the store's several restaurants. This one's offerings included pecan chicken salad on raisin bread. It was overly fussy for Ab's taste. Nevertheless, he rotated through them all for his daily lunch, chewing and keeping an eye peeled for trouble or staff laxness.

"I usually do the nose punching," I assured him. "I miss the sandwiches though. I should remember to come here more often."

Ab and I got along better now than when I'd worked with him. I'd started part-time at Rike's when I was sixteen, emptying trash and running errands, then working full time as a floorwalker and eventually in loss prevention. That was at the bottom of the Depression. Ab hadn't been the only one who thought it was wrong to give work to a woman when so many men with families couldn't get a job. Now he hired me on a retainer to run background checks on potential employees.

"What have you heard about the trouble up the street?" I indicated with my head.

"Trouble?"

His eyes snapped to full attention.

"At Lagarde Jewelry. I saw police cars in front. One belongs to the homicide boys."

"Homicide! Maybe there was a robbery and something went wrong." He fingered a bushy mustache. "Word would have filtered up by now, though, don't you think?"

"You'd think."

When an accident or a fire occurred nearby, customers came in chattering. The news rose from street level through all seven floors faster than the store's escalator.

"You wouldn't happen to be working on something involving the place, would you?" Ab crumpled his napkin on the table.

"I'm hoping Lagarde can give me some help with something I'm working on. I understand he's an expert at spotting copies."

"That he is. We even had him take a look at something we got in once. It might have been while you were still here."

We left the restaurant. I knew by his direction we were headed back to his office.

"Let's ask Vivian if she's heard anything."

She was his secretary, and in our absence she'd heard there were police cars in front of Lagarde Jewelry. That was all.

"If I get wind of anything, want me to give you a call?" Ab asked as he walked with me to the stairs.

"I'd appreciate it. I'll be out a lot, though, so I may stop in to see you."

I took my leave and stopped on the way downstairs to chat with a clerk or two I'd worked with. I spent some time in the book department, then in hats. My hope was that the cop cars down the street would have disappeared by the time I left, allowing me to mosey down the street and stick my nose in.

When I went out the Ludlow Street exit and glanced that way, Freeze's unmarked car was gone but two patrol cars were still in evidence. Pretending to study a window display of ladies fashions, I debated my next move. Did I dare stroll down and shoot the breeze with the uniforms? I took a peep and got my answer. A blocky figure had appeared and now stood talking to a pair of beat cops.

Boike.

I swung my gaze back to the fashion display just as the detective glanced around. And possibly saw me.

For the next several minutes I studied the clothing on the mannequins before me avidly. Especially the hats. I mulled over the shoes. I looked up at the hats. I shifted position and pursed my lips thoughtfully. All the while, I watched the glass. When I was starting to hope the coast might be clear, I caught sight of Boike's reflection.

"You never struck me as the type to drool over dresses," he greeted.

"Are you kidding? If I was rolling in dough, I'd have a closet full. Is Freeze letting you off to go shopping these days?" I looked in the direction of the patrol cars. "Oh, jeez. Were you at that jewelry store? Did somebody try to rob the place?"

His manner switched from curiosity to alertness.

"What do you know about it?"

"Just that there's a fancy one down there. Some Frenchie name."

"I don't suppose anyone there's ever been a client of yours."

"No. I worked here before I hung out my shingle. Used to walk past... *was* there a robbery?"

Boike relaxed some.

"Nah. A stiff in the alley."

"Somebody who worked there?"

He clamped his mouth shut.

"Come on, Boike. Can you at least tell me if it was the same as the girl who got strangled behind The Canterbury?"

Boike considered. He was more reasonable than his boss. A sense of fair play was probably telling him I had a right to know that much.

"Only in that they're both dead," he said. "Anyway, it's starting to look like that girl behind the hotel got killed by her boyfriend. He hopped a freight out of town around then. We'll probably never know if he meant to kill her or they had a fight."

Did his answer mean the new body in the alley belonged to a man? That the victim hadn't been strangled? That the victim hadn't been an employee of the jewelry store?

Maybe it only meant two people were dead.

* * *

Having worked at Rike's meant I knew exactly where every pay phone was located. As soon as Boike left I bolted inside to the nearest one. With luck I could talk to the jewelry store before he got back and told anyone he'd seen me. If Freeze was down there, he was likely to put the kibosh on anyone except cops answering phone calls.

"Lagarde Jewelry," a subdued voice answered. A female voice. Good.

"Oh, hello," I fluttered. "I talked to Mr. Lagarde last week about a bracelet that's been in our family for ages, and he said I should bring it by so he could look at it. If I stop by in half an hour or so, will he be available?"

"I'm... afraid not."

The strain in the voice made me ninety percent certain.

"Tomorrow, then?" I asked brightly.

Silence.

Maybe this was the first time she'd had to break the news. Maybe she'd had to break it so often it was taking its toll.

"Mr. Lagarde..." She cleared her throat. "Mr. Lagarde passed away over the weekend."

TWENTY-ONE

The murder of the jeweler and the hotel scrub girl were connected. I was sure of it. Even though it would spare The Canterbury further scrutiny, and mean my client was no longer suspected of murder, I didn't buy the idea that Polly had died at the hands of a boyfriend who'd skipped town. Her death, and Lagarde's, had something to do what now appeared to be definite breaches of the hotel safe.

I drove back to my office, but I didn't go in. Instead I walked a block and a half to where I knew I'd find a ragged towhead kid selling papers.

"Hey, sis." He broke into a gap-tooth grin at sight of me. "You been sick? I ain't— haven't seen you."

"Working someplace else for a week or so, early and late."

"And you missed me, huh?"

Heebs was ten or eleven. He lived on the streets. He was smart as a whip, and always pestering to be my assistant.

"Yeah, Heebs, I did. Got a job for you too, if you're interested."

"You know it. What's the story?"

When it wouldn't expose him to anything dangerous, I occasionally found a task for him and paid him a pittance. I gave him a dime to cover the two papers left in his sack. If he still got a chance to sell them after we'd talked, it was okay by me.

"I need you to find out who uses the alley behind a hotel called The Canterbury."

I told him where it was. As long as he'd knocked around on his own, he knew more about who slept in certain doorways and dug through certain trash cans than I did. What he didn't know, he could learn by asking a pal, who might have to ask his own pal, but eventually I'd get what I needed

"How much you going to gouge me for?" I asked.

He grinned again.

"Ah, sis, you know I'd do it for nothing. You can give me whatever you want."

"A buck when you deliver. I'll stop by tomorrow."

* * *

My building didn't have a doorman in a fancy uniform, but it did have an elevator. The thought of riding up to my fourth floor office sounded appealing, what with all the running up and down stairs I'd been doing at The Canterbury. Before I reached it, the metal gate banged close.

"Wait, please," I called.

My hand hit the button to keep the car from starting up accidentally.

It didn't budge.

The grill didn't open, either.

A pruned faced woman stared back at me from the other side.

"You'll have to wait for it to come back," she said primly. "You'll bend my sign."

"Nice to see you, too, Maxine."

She and her husband owned a sock wholesale place down the hall from my office. Maxine didn't like me much. It was mutual. Her sign, mounted on a wooden stick, wasn't quite as wide as the elevator, but it was good-sized. *KEEP OUR BOYS HOME*, it said.

The fact she was an isolationist didn't surprise me. The fact she was willing to stand on a street corner waving a sign did. She was dressed in black and her hat had a veil that could be pulled down, the uniform of women across the country who took part in the so-called Mother's Movement. They spit on members of Congress who didn't share their views and had hanged one Senator in effigy.

"You do know the Selective Service Act passed, don't you, Maxine?"

"If we stop that nasty Mr. Roosevelt from being elected again, it won't matter. And we will. We'll defeat him. Mrs. Lindbergh's on our side and she knows what it's like to lose a son!"

Letting a count's flunky keep me out of a hotel elevator was one thing. I wasn't going to put up with the same treatment in my own building. My hand hadn't budged from the button. Maxine still held the folding gate stubbornly closed. Since she was twice my age, it didn't seem fair to tussle with her physically. Not when I had a better idea.

"Since you asked so nicely, I'll let you have it all to yourself," I said.

Releasing the button, I raced for the stairs. One floor up, I sidetracked to the elevator and hit the UP button that would make it stop and open its doors. Then I ran some more.

By the time the elevator arrived on four, I stood, somewhat out of breath, directly in front of it. My outstretched arms, braced on the wall at either side, blocked Maxine's exit.

"We can play this game all day, if you want," I said. "Or, if you have better things to do, you can ride back down and come up the stairs like I did."

The woman looked ready to have a conniption. Finally her hand smacked the DOWN button and the car descended.

It took her longer to get up the stairs than it had me. When I caught sight of the top of her sign bobbling into view, I went down the hall to my office. Nobody had fixed the window shade yet. It still hung drunkenly. I thought of whacking it off with scissors. Then I had a better idea.

Since the cops apparently were looking elsewhere for Polly's killer, this seemed like the perfect time to visit the neighborhood where she'd lived.

* * *

"Polly Bunten? I already told the police every lick I know. Ask them."

The sloppy old biddy who'd been Polly's landlady started to slam the door. I blocked it with my hip.

"I'm asking you." I shoved my license under her nose. "But if you don't feel chatty, there are people at City Hall I can have a swell talk with about what a safety hazard your place is."

It didn't look much worse than some of its neighbors. Houses along the narrow street southwest of the bus station hadn't seen paint since the bottom dropped out of things. Roofs had patches. Porches sagged.

"I do the best I can," the woman sniveled. Her dress had stains on it. Yellowish particles clung to the wrinkled handkerchief she brought out. "I'm a widow—"

"Yeah, fine. Show me Polly's room." If I could find out about the boyfriend Boike had mentioned, maybe I could start connecting some dots.

"It's rented again." The landlady fell back a step as I stared. "Rent was due Saturday. I've got to eat, don't I?" she said defensively.

I had trouble prying my jaws open.

"What did you do with her things?"

"Sold 'em to a second hand place. Polly was always borrowing milk for her brat, and she sure isn't going to pay me back now, is she? You got any more questions, ask the woman down at that brown house."

She slammed the door while I stood stunned by the revelation Polly Bunten, whom Francis had described as a kid, had a child herself.

* * *

"I'm trying to find out about Polly Bunten," I said to the woman who opened the door at what I'd finally determined must be the "brown house". From directly in front, patches of color were visible along the corners and in a sheltered strip under the stoop roof.

The woman's face drooped at mention of Polly. She looked thirty, but was possibly younger.

"Who are you? Why are you asking?" she asked warily.

"My name's Maggie Sullivan. I'm a private investigator." I heard her breath catch. "The couple who own the hotel where Polly worked asked me to see what I could find out about her. If she had family and that. They'd like to do whatever they can."

Her sweater was darned in a dozen places, but she was as tidy as the landlady had been slovenly. Her hand stroked the head of a toddler who peered around her skirt.

"I'm Bess," she said after a moment. I guess you might as well come in."

Her small front room was a tidy as she was. An older boy pushed a long wooden block around, making train noises. At a gesture, I sat on a daybed that served as a couch. Bedding was folded on one end.

"Could I get you some tea?" Bess plucked nervously at the arm of her sweater.

"No thanks." It was clear she didn't need hospitality depleting what little she had in the way of groceries. "I could sure use some water, though."

That seemed to relax her.

"How old are the boys?" I asked when she returned from the kitchen. I didn't spend much time looking at kids.

"Two and three. The one on the floor's my brother's boy. He and his wife moved in when he lost his job. They both work part time now. I watch the kids.

"It's nice someone cared about Polly. Asking after her family. I don't think she had any, though, except for Ella."

"Her little girl?"

She nodded.

"Looked like a fairy princess, and sweet as they come. Polly would carry her over wrapped up in a quilt. We'd put her on one of the daybed cushions down on the floor there, so Polly could slip in and pick her up when she got home. Most of the time the little mite didn't even wake up."

Bess sighed and cuddled the toddler who'd crawled into her lap.

"I'd have loved to keep her after - after Polly died. But we barely get by as it is. The police... well, I guess that awful old woman where Polly lived told you they'd been around asking questions. They sent for a woman from a home where they take tots like Ella. I guess if Polly's employers wanted to send some money there, for her to have a dolly or something, it would cheer her at least.

"Oh, and maybe they could take this." Jumping up, she took a snapshot from on top of a cheap clock that sat on a cabinet and handed it to me. "It may help Ella remember her when she gets older."

I looked down at the image of an incredibly pretty young woman.

"Who took this?"

"Some friend of Jerry's – her boyfriend." For the first time since I'd met her, she teared up. "There's no way to reach him. Let him know what happened. He took it into his head that if he went to Iowa or one of those places out there, he'd find work. Had a cousin or something. Polly just about cried her eyes out."

"When did he leave?"

She dabbed at her eyes with a fresh white hanky.

"Two, three weeks ago? About when Polly started her job."

Well before she'd been killed then.

"Are you sure?"

Bess nodded. "Like I said, Polly just about cried her eyes out. They both did."

TWENTY-TWO

"Yeah, that was Jerry's girl. I never knew her name," said a customer who'd come up to pay for a bar of Lifebuoy soap as I was showing the owner of a neighborhood grocery store Polly's picture.

The store was a block from where the dead girl had lived. It stuck to the basics: Bread, butter, eggs. And milk. If Polly had gotten milk for her little girl, I'd figured she'd most likely come here.

"When was the last time you saw Jerry?" I asked.

The man, a big fellow in a flannel shirt and overalls, rubbed a stubble of beard as he squinted in thought.

"Two weeks ago last Friday. Payday. I was headed to a joint I like for a beer before I went into work. I'm on night shift. Place I go to, the back of it's so close to the tracks you could practically spit on the trains. I was cutting though that way, and there was him and the girl with their arms wrapped around each other. I started to call to them – you know, kid. Then I saw they was both crying like their hearts would break."

"Any idea why?"

It was the first real information I'd unearthed since leaving Bess' place.

"Not right then. Jerry was trying to give her some money, but she said no, he'd need it to get by. He shoved it in her pocket and said he wanted her to have it in case the baby got sick. Then a freight came rolling toward us and I couldn't hear any more. He kissed her real hard and turned and ran and grabbed for a boxcar. I tell you, I held my breath for a second, but then I saw him haul himself in."

The grocery store owner was so caught up in the tale that his lips were parted.

"And you're sure that was two weeks ago?"

The customer laid his bar of soap on the counter along with some money. He rubbed his stubble again.

"Wasn't this last Friday, and the one before that, my wife's family was all packed in our place celebrating her sister's birthday. So yeah, two weeks."

* * *

I made the rounds of three beer joints. What I picked up there confirmed the story of the customer with the soap. Jerry hadn't been seen in two weeks or more. He'd been heading west to find work.

Polly's boyfriend wasn't the one who'd killed her.

I went to my office to think about who had.

Whoever it was, it now seemed all but certain that Polly had died because she'd seen something. Something to do with the hotel safe. When I'd tossed my hat on the rack, I took out the list of hotel employees I'd left there on Saturday.

I'd already eliminated the recently fired bartender, the only employee with grudge enough against the Tuckers to try and steal from them. He'd been laid up with food poisoning. True, he could have hired someone to break into the safe, but getting in would require expertise. In addition to skill, a safe cracker would need knowledge of the hotel's layout and schedules. The idea of a partner was too farfetched to entice me.

That left the second most likely candidate, Len Welles, his breezy replacement. A paperclip held Len's application to a couple of reference letters.

Birch Lodge was the name he'd listed as his last employer. A note in the margin said 'went out of business.' That matched what he'd said when he'd flirted with me in the bar. It was also a dandy way to prevent anyone from checking. Still, at least I could check to see if the place had existed.

It was somewhere in Michigan. I dialed the operator and gave her the name of the town and asked for the number. There was some back and forth between her and another operator about what exchange it was on, but eventually they came up with one. When I called, however, the number rang and rang.

While waiting for inspiration to strike, I noticed my manicure had begun to look shopworn. I got out a bottle of polish remover and took off the color. I walked upstairs to the Ladies and washed my hands. Then I did some filing. The kind with an emery board. Then I gave my nails two coats of polish. By the time I'd finished, I'd also had an idea.

Fitting the unsharpened pencil I kept for such purposes into the bottom hole of the telephone dial, I swept the dial around in a circle.

"Op-uh-ray-tuh."

I asked for the post office in the burg where Birch Lodge was located. Another minute or two and it was ringing.

"Post Office," answered a cheerful woman. At any rate she sounded jolly.

"I'm calling from Ohio," I said. "Are you the postmistress?"

She laughed merrily.

"No, dear, that's my husband. He came in early and took off early to get in an hour of fishing. Could I help you?"

"Sure," I said. "At least I hope so. Birch Lodge. When did it go out of business?"

"Dear me. It would be four or five months ago now. Right at the start of the season. The owners were sure they could turn things around, what with times getting better. But the bank had extended their loan too many times already, I guess. Were you needing to reach someone there?"

"No, no. A man who's applied for a job said he used to work there. My boss asked me to check."

"It wouldn't be that nice young Len, would it? Len Welles?"

"Why, yes it would."

"Lovely young fellow. And now that I think, he was from Ohio, wasn't he? I'm sure he left a forwarding address if you'd like me to look—"

"No, that's fine." Every minute of chat was adding to my telephone bill. "You've been very helpful. I hope your husband, uh, catches big fish."

She laughed as if I'd said something funny.

Maybe I had.

Three hours and numerous phone calls later, I'd eliminated the desk clerks, the bellboys, the doorman and half the dining room staff as likely suspects. No one owed large sums of money. Except for a single fine for running a stop sign, none had gotten themselves in trouble. Former employers and landlords sang their praises.

I needed a drink.

TWENTY-THREE

What I actually wanted was to walk into Finn's and have Wee Willie give me a hard time. Instead I returned to The Canterbury. As much as Tucker fought the idea, it was time to take a look at his guests. A few of them had been around when his safe troubles started. Besides, if I went to Finn's, I'd only run the risk of Connelly's bringing his ladylove in.

Frances was leaving the desk with a sheaf of papers in hand when I entered the lobby. She veered to join me.

"Maybe you're not as smart as I thought if you're sticking around." Her smile was lopsided. "Joshua told me about the appraiser."

"There's more."

I told her about Lagarde's death as we ambled along. She absorbed it with the stoicism of one grown numb to bad news. But when I mentioned Polly's daughter, she gasped. Her eyes filled with tears.

"That *child* had a baby?"

"Yes."

Hugging the papers against her, she shook her head. Her lips were pressed together.

"Where... what will become of her? The baby."

"They took her to an orphanage."

The intensity of her response startled me. I opened my purse.

"Polly's friend thought you might want to take them this picture of Polly, for when the girl's older. Maybe take a toy or something for her. Here's the address."

Frances nodded wordlessly. I told her I was going to start taking a look at hotel guests.

"We trust your judgment," she said absently, and went on her way.

We'd ended up at the little conversation area of chairs and couches. A foursome waited by the elevator.

"Forget bath salts. I need horse liniment," one moaned.

Mitzi, her white-blonde tresses hidden under a turban-style hat, rested her back against the wall as if she might at any moment slide down it.

One of the others muttered a comment and all of them laughed. The dancers, it appeared, had just returned from rehearsing.

Cheered by the thought my afternoon might not have been so bad in comparison, I went into the lounge and folded my arms on the bar. Since it seemed a waste not to have something fancier than what I could mix for myself, I once again asked for a martini.

"Put hers on my bill." Loren Avery had come up behind me. "Please. It's the least I can do," he said as I started to protest.

"For what?"

"Being such a good sport when Mother was playing cupid. And whiskey for me, Len. Make it a double. Join me?" He indicated a table. Sinking into a chair, he closed his eyes briefly and threw his head back.

"Rough day?"

"I've had better." The choreographer gave a wry smile. "Worse too, probably. I knew I'd have my work cut out trying to get an actress who's never done so much as a shuffle step to pass as a dancer. What I didn't expect was for her to have two left feet and no ear for rhythm. How about your day?"

I wasn't used to anyone asking.

"Okay. I, um, got lots of measurements organized."

Len left the bar to set our drinks before us.

"Economy of motion, that's what your work boils down to, doesn't it?" Loren mused when he'd sipped some whiskey. "You see it in good dancers, too." Something caught his attention. "Nick! Come join us."

The man reputed to move from one rich woman to another strolled over with hands in his pockets. He was handsome, all right, and had that air of mockery which some of my gender found attractive.

"Back from the salt mines, are you?" Nick sat down and snapped his fingers to summon Len. Apparently good looks eliminated the need for manners.

"Have you met Miss Sullivan?" Loren asked.

Although he hadn't, the other man nodded. His eyes flicked over me without interest. Nice to know my fortune was safe.

"Did someone tell me you were here visiting your grandma?" I asked brightly.

"Great-aunt." He turned toward Loren.

"What's her name?" I persisted. "Maybe I know her."

He didn't like it, but he couldn't ignore me without seeming rude.

"Clara Drake," he said smoothly. Taking out a gold lighter chased with his initial, he lighted up and blew smoke in my direction.

"Drake… Drake…." I tapped my chin. "What was her husband's name?"

"Carlton. Owned part of a railroad."

I listened with half an ear while the two men talked. What little I'd seen of Nick Perry, beginning with the scrap with Lena, had made me dislike him. It didn't make him a crook. Still, he was the one who'd lured Loren Avery and the Hollywood set to Dayton. He conveniently had a relative here and just happened to be visiting her at the same time.

Suddenly Loren muttered under his breath.

"There's Archie. No doubt wanting a glowing report on the day's activities and ready to snap my head off if I don't give one. Excuse me a minute."

He pushed back from the table.

"Gee, he's a friendly fellow," I said.

"Just swell." Nick snapped his fingers to summon another drink.

The lounge was scantily populated. The three men here for meetings with Boss Kett stood at the bar sipping what looked like whiskey. I'd watched others order, then carry their glasses to tables.

Nick picked up his lighter again.

"So. You're doing some sort of work for the hotel, are you? Toddling around with your little ruler."

"Yes, time-motion analysis. You'd be amazed how much it can help a business trim expenses."

"Do tell." His lighter snapped. He exhaled in my direction, watching to see if I'd turn my head. "Smart women bore me."

"Oh, don't worry when they're brainier than you," I said earnestly. "I'm sure they're perfectly happy if you're a good dancer and hold their wrap for them and things like that."

The man across from me stared, his face darkening. He snatched the cigarette from his mouth to respond.

"There you are, sir." Len set the requested drink in front of him and whisked away empties. "Another for you, miss?" The bartender's eye held a glint of mischief as it connected with mine.

"No, thanks. I've got to run. I'm meeting some friends."

As I rose to leave someone sideswiped me from behind. It was Lena. Oblivious to me, she shook a note on hotel paper under Nick's nose.

"You can't seriously expect me to traipse along to this – this music recital with the two of you tomorrow!"

"You don't want Great Auntie to be disappointed, do you?"

"You could have made some excuse, surely! It's bad enough we have to spend extra time in this dump. Now we have to spend all afternoon—"

"I'm no happier about the delay than you are. It's not my doing. Would you rather sit around and make conversation with the narrow-minded old witch? This is only for a couple of hours."

They'd lowered their voices, but thanks to the half wall separating lounge from lobby, I could hear without dawdling much as I made my exit.

"Sigmund Romberg!" snapped Lena. "I hate every sticky-sweet song he ever wrote!"

She stormed out behind me.

* * *

I wanted a good, dark glass of stout and the sound of familiar voices around me. I headed to Finn's. It had been my place a long time before it was Connelly's, and I was going to sit and enjoy myself no matter what.

Wee Willie had already finished his pint and headed home to his wife and kids by the time I arrived. Some of the regulars at the long bar along one side of the room greeted me as I passed. Rose was working the taps while Finn hauled a crate of something in from the back. As I slid onto a stool, she bustled over.

"I'll bring your pint, love. Go on over there. Something must have gone terrible wrong in Chicago. Poor lamb didn't say two words when he came in. He looks like his heart's fit to break."

A bob of her head indicated Connelly at a table alone. His shoulders were slumped.

I hadn't had the best of days either, but nobody seemed to care. Except maybe Loren Avery, who'd at least had manners to ask. I opened my mouth to tell Rose as much.

"Where's Seamus?" I asked instead.

"Hasn't been in. Him or Billy either."

I looked at Connelly again. His dark brown head with its glints of red was bowed in misery. I swallowed. Connelly deserved to be happy. If a chance at that had been snatched away, the least I could do was give him some sympathy.

The sound of a chair scraping back brought him out of his reverie.

"Mind some company?"

A long moment passed before his head shook once.

"Don't know that you'll find any in me." He tossed back the last of his Guinness.

Rose was sliding mine in front of me, and setting down a replacement for Connelly's, before I'd even settled in my seat.

"Doesn't look like your trip went that well," I observed after we'd sipped in silence.

He propped his elbows on the table and grunted.

"Worst couple of days I've had this side of the ocean. We'd agreed a price. Talked long distance. The fellow swore he'd sell to no other. Then when I got there, the s.o.b had. Some swell who works for the mayor had come along and offered more money."

Something was way off track here.

"You talked like you were going there to meet a girl," I said carefully.

He frowned.

"Why would I care about meeting a girl? In Chicago or anyplace else?" Leaning across his folded arms he spoke with an excitement he expected me to share. "I'd found pipes, Maggie. A year and more of looking, and finally I got word of somebody selling a set of pipes! Blackwood... ivory fittings. Fine, fine work, too. I'd heard a set by the same maker played in Boston." He raked a hand through his hair. "Ah, Maggie, I could practically feel them on my knee!"

I'd have laughed if he hadn't looked so miserable.

"I'm sorry, Connelly."

I knew he meant uilleann pipes, not Scottish. They were scarce as hen's teeth. I thought of my dad's set, how he'd held them, how he'd lost himself in the music. A wave of caring swept me for the man across the table. I could make him so happy just by driving across town. Just by facing Maeve Murphy. Only I couldn't.

I pushed back, desperate to flee my own feelings. And memories. And myself. Connelly's gaze suddenly sharpened.

"What happened to your neck?"

Somewhere along the way, the scarf intended to hide the evidence of last night's attack had slipped. I tugged it up.

"Tree branch hit me." Before he could question further, I got to my feet. "Have things to do, but I'm glad you're back safe."

I touched his shoulder in passing. His hand came up to cover mine, welding us not with the dangerous current any contact usually sparked, but with something deeper I couldn't explain. I felt a curious urge to caress the back of his head.

TWENTY-FOUR

"Last night when I asked, you said the only thing in the safe besides jewelry was passports."

"That's right." Tucker eyed me alertly.

It was after dinner. I'd gone up to their apartment.

"You've thought of something," said Frances.

"Maybe."

Something was bothering me. The man who'd disappeared. The envelope. How did that fit everything else that had happened? What was I missing?

I turned to her husband.

"The day you saw the empty box in the safe. You told me no one had wanted anything from the safe except for Count Szarenski getting his passport."

"Right."

"Does he do that often?"

"Every morning. Well, except Sunday. Takes it out and a couple hours later puts it back in."

"The envelope that was left behind when that man disappeared, was it big enough to hold a passport?"

"Maybe." The hotel owner looked uncertain. "Bigger than what you'd need for a letter, at least. But the address he gave – it was in Indiana."

"And it was phony."

"Right."

Frances cocked her head with interest. I got up to pace.

"What do you need a passport for? Besides getting in and out of a country?"

"Cashing checks. Anything official, where you'd need to prove who you were." Tucker tugged at his earlobe. "Renting an apartment, maybe. Buying something big, like a house or... I don't know. A business? Shares in one?"

He looked to Frances for further ideas.

"Opening a credit account at a store? So his wife could buy clothes?"

My prowling had brought me close to the window where Frances had stood when the two of us waited for updates on the discovery of Polly's body. I could just make out the river in the distance. Why would the count need his passport every morning? That was a lot of checks to cash or things to buy.

"Does Szarenski take anyone with him when he goes out?"

"His man. That Bartoz fellow."

"Does Bartoz get his passport too?"

"No. Just the count."

"Same time every morning?"

"More or less. Ten-thirty, eleven. Kind of a pain, to tell you the truth, 'cause we're busy with people checking out. You getting an idea?"

I had a couple.

Nick Perry had turned up just as the Hollywood crowd with their jewelry started arriving. The count had made his appearance around the time the missing man vanished. Which branch of the path should I follow?

* * *

At my request, the night clerk called to wake me at midnight. The bar closed then. Night owl guests would head for their rooms. The place would be settling down, meaning I'd have a chance to talk to the other two scrub women. Under guise of evaluating how the night crew performed their functions, of course.

I didn't learn much.

The two women who'd worked with Polly were post-middle age, their knees already failing. They were both built like feed sacks. They came in at midnight and left at four-thirty in the morning.

They started on the top floor and worked their way down. They cleaned woodwork; polished every inch of the considerable brass affixed to the elevator, which was locked and inoperable from half-past midnight to six; got down on their hands and knees to buff the wood peeking out at the edges of the carpeting covering the winding front staircase. Anything which was noiseless and didn't require full lighting, they did at night. They spoke to each other in whispers.

The women also cleaned the back stairs used by staff. "If you tried it daytime, you'd get nothing done but move out of their way," one explained. When they finished the second floor, two continued down the back stairs into the cavernous kitchen where their brushes and pails full of hot water freed its floor of that day's spills. The third woman saw to the lobby where she dusted and waxed the front desk. Last of all, she scrubbed the floor in the lounge.

Most of the time the women took turns, but since Polly was new, they'd been letting her finish up on the lobby and lounge so she didn't have to learn the kitchen part yet.

If that didn't confirm my theory that the girl had seen someone coming out of Tucker's office, it certainly strengthened it.

* * *

For once I was able to avail myself of the hotel's luxuries, sleeping late and enjoying a room service breakfast after my bath. Their oatmeal wasn't quite up to McCrory's.

Since I wanted to be in place well ahead of when Count Szarenski and his muscle usually collected his passport, and had several things to ask Tucker if I came across him, I got downstairs shortly before nine. Nick Perry was just going out the front door.

Something clicked. Perry had been out early the day I'd witness his row with Lena. Maybe he just liked a morning walk, but even that could be worth knowing.

"Shove this somewhere." I thrust the book with which I'd planned to while away time into Smith's startled hands. "If Count Szarenski goes out, tell me what time and which direction."

The old bellhop nodded.

Perry was half a block away by the time I reached the street. A good distance for following. Mercifully he showed no inclination to head for a trolley or flag a taxi.

After walking another block, he glanced back. I studied a shop window. Perry moved with the swift stride of a man who knew where he was headed. He didn't look back again.

The better part of town began to give way to inexpensive clothing stores, dry goods shops and small cafes. I'd been behind Perry long enough he might notice me if he looked back again. Crossing the street I went into the entry of a place that repaired vacuum sweepers. I pulled a rolled up cloche from my purse and put it on, then shook out a thin muslin shopping bag and dropped my purse inside. I'd packed the quick-change for when I tagged after the count. Unless a man was up to no good and exceptionally jittery, it wouldn't occur to him I might be the same woman he'd seen earlier.

Now I stuck to the side of the street across from Perry. I closed the gap between us a bit; paused to look in a shop window; repeated. The man I was watching halted. He looked up as if checking numbers. He turned up a set of steps into what I could see, as I moseyed up my side, was a secondhand store.

It didn't strike me as the sort of place the finely dressed Mr. Perry would buy clothing.

"Hey, I need shoelaces. Got any gray ones?" I asked, ducking into a shop that advertised leather repair. Its small window held a display of creams and brushes and gave a dandy view of the place across the way.

"Gray? Never heard of gray shoelaces," frowned the white-haired proprietor. He wiped his hands absently on a leather apron. "Got black, or how about these nice tan ones? They'd go good. What length?"

"Four eyelets. I'm sure I've seen gray."

He walked to the back of the narrow space where he bent to talk to a woman doing something with glue. The smell of it stabbed at the space just above the bridge of my nose. As the shoe repairman made his way back, Nick Perry emerged from the secondhand store. He hadn't stayed long and he wasn't carrying anything.

"Wife says she's never heard of gray shoelaces," the old guy reported.

"I guess I better take these tan ones, then."

I wanted Perry to get down the street some before I went out. By the time I'd paid for the shoelaces, he was well on his way, and by the looks of it headed back to the hotel. I trotted across to the secondhand store.

The inside was dusted and polished. Displays here and there were done nicely enough to grace the windows at Rike's. A middle-aged woman who was perched on a stool at a display case smiled and murmured a greeting. She returned to writing prices on tags.

The top of the display case held a far-from-new cash register. The glassed in part below held assorted jewelry. It was a cut or two above the dime store kind, to my untrained eye, but from the prices indicated on each piece, far from real.

It was early for customers, but I took a fast turn up and down the aisles. No one else was in evidence. At the back, a curtain hid what was probably storage and a washroom. No rustle of boxes met my ears; no footsteps. I went back up front.

"Oh, gee, you don't have that pin that looked like a bird anymore."

"Like a bird?"

The woman writing out price tags looked up. Bending my knees, I pretended to search the display case.

"It was here last week. That guy who just left didn't buy it, did he?"

The woman frowned in perplexity.

"Why, no. He bought a rhinestone bracelet."

TWENTY-FIVE

"Guy you need to talk to's named Punchy MacKenzie," Heebs told me between selling papers.

"Got his name 'cause he mixes whatever dribbles he finds in liquor bottles together to get him a drink. Doesn't sound safe to me, what with TB and such."

"You're right about that."

By the time I left the secondhand store, I'd lost sight of Perry. Whether he'd returned to the hotel or gone somewhere else, the purchase he'd just made was interesting enough. I'd decided if I took a cab back to the hotel parking lot and then drove, I could touch base with Heebs and still be back to watch for Szarenski, so I had.

"This Punchy sober enough of the time for me to trust what he says?" I asked.

Heebs grinned and paused to sell another paper. He dropped the pennies he'd gotten into his money pouch with fleeting disappointment. No tip.

"The kid that gave me his name says he is. Says Punchy usually tries to get fed at the soup kitchen on Fifth the other side of Bainbridge. The one by that church with the busted window. Gets in line around five."

He conducted another business transaction. This time the customer let him keep the whole nickel. Thanked him, too.

"Look for a skinny guy with a gold tooth." Heebs indicated an eyetooth. "He must be tough if nobody's knocked it out to sell it, huh? You need a bodyguard?"

I stuffed the dollar I'd promised plus a little extra into his pocket and winked.

"That's your prime time for selling the evening edition. I'll manage. If anyone gets out of line, I'll mention your name. That should make them back off."

The sound of the kid's laugh made my steps lighter as I walked away.

* * *

I'd parked my DeSoto in the hotel lot and was reaching to turn the ignition off when I spotted the count and his aide de camp leaving the hotel. I thanked whatever saints might still listen to me that I hadn't missed them. Once the two were safely past, I got out and followed.

This round of fox and hound moved more slowly than the one with Nick Perry. Count Szarenski had a cane, but he didn't lean on it much. He merely moved with deliberation.

The positions of the pair interested me. Bartoz walked one step behind the older man and at his right elbow. Close enough to exchange a few words, but not like equals. Was it some remnant of their culture? Or… was Bartoz protecting the old man? I realized he was making frequent checks of their surroundings, albeit subtly.

Their activities weren't the kind ordinarily associated with danger. They went to a bank. I watched through the window. As nearly as I could tell, no money changed hands. Their next stop was the post office. Even if I got out my hat and shopping bag, the chance of being recognized was too great for me to risk following.

A woman with a seamed face started up the steps. She had some unstamped letters in her hand. I touched her sleeve.

"Excuse me. That fellow with the cane who just went in, he's my uncle. If he picks up a package it's going to spoil the surprise we've got planned for his birthday. If I wait over there, could you let me know if he does?"

She nodded and smiled.

A short time later Szarenski and Bartoz came out. I was well past the entrance, turned away and pretending to powder my nose so I could use the mirror in the lid of my compact to watch. The count's shoulders looked to me like they were slumped. When the pair had gone on, I snapped the compact closed and went inside.

The woman I'd talked to was folding half a dozen stamps she'd bought into a piece of Cut-Rite. She noticed me and her eyes twinkled in conspiracy.

"He went to the counter. I think he asked about mail, but they didn't give him anything."

"Oh, good." I puffed out my cheeks, dramatizing relief. "The party's not spoiled, then."

* * *

Count Szarenski was waiting for something. That was my guess if he was making these same stops every morning, which, judging by the schedule Tucker had described, he was.

Package?

Letter?

Maybe. Except...

The only thing you got at a bank was money.

Nick Perry, on the other hand, had picked up a rhinestone bracelet on his morning rambles. Could the two men be allied in some way I was missing? Or were they two different trains on parallel tracks?

I wanted to find out more about Perry. I wanted to find out more about Count Szarenski. And I knew a woman who could probably do a pretty good job of wrecking trains.

TWENTY-SIX

Rachel Minsky slid a three-page form across the table to me. We were in a booth at a working-class restaurant on Watervliet that served cabbage rolls, which Rachel said were Hungarian. The dark beer we were drinking while we waited wasn't half bad. Apart from a waitress, we were the only women, but no one in the noonday crowd so much as ogled us. It strongly suggested Rachel was known here.

"You mind telling me why you wanted a bid sheet for a construction project? And why couldn't you pick it up at my office?" she asked.

Rachel looked like a porcelain doll: pointed chin, a cloud of dark hair, pulp magazine bosom. The suit she had on had set her back more than I paid for a month's rent. A trio of minks chased each other around her neck. She could have fit right in with the guests at the Canterbury, except, perhaps, for the fact that she was a Jew. And ran a construction company. And, somewhere -- ever so discreetly -- carried a gun.

She was the black ewe in a family that otherwise ran to bankers and lawyers and women who stayed home. Plenty of people claimed she was crooked. I trusted her.

"I need a form that looks semi-official if nobody reads too closely. I'm kind of short on time, and I figured if you'd meet me for lunch it would save some."

"And?"

"And I thought if I plied you with liquor, I might pry useful information out of you," I said.

"A man here and there has tried that." She cocked her head. "Are your intentions pure?"

I grinned.

Rachel's eyes were dark as an abyss. As dangerous to misjudge, too. Right now they suggested amusement. She took out a tortoiseshell lighter and matching cigarette case.

"What kind of information you need?"

"Didn't you tell me once your people were Polish?"

"My family, you mean? Way back when. My mother's side had been here ten, fifteen years before she was born. My father was a toddler when his folks came over."

"You know much about the politics there?"

"Apart from Hitler taking over? Not really. Near as I can tell, their history's pretty much been fight, lose, get gobbled up by some country, then repeat the whole thing with another country gobbling them. Why?"

"I need to find out about a man named Szarenski. Whether he's really a count, for starters."

She was fitting a cigarette into a long gold holder. Her head snapped up.

"He's real, all right. War hero. He fought against the Nazis when they rolled in, then joined an underground group. Home Army or some such. The Germans burned his estate, killed a relative – brother, son."

She shrugged off her display of knowledge.

"My father and brothers talk about things over there at Shabbat dinner. The women start talking kids. I drift in and out." Lighting the cigarette, she jutted her jaw to the side so the smoke she expelled didn't reach me. She studied me thoughtfully. "Don't tell me something you're working on involves Szarenski."

"Not directly."

I paused while the waitress served our cabbage rolls. When we were alone again, I outlined the situation, omitting the fact I had my eye on the count as a suspect.

"The mere fact he would come here instead of a bigger city seems... odd." Rachel rocked the paw of a dead mink back and forth in her fingers. "It would be kind of fun knowing something my brothers don't. Let me see what I can find out."

* * *

Before putting Rachel's nifty form to work, I wanted to pursue another idea. Suppose, I thought, that no jewelry ever appeared to be missing from the hotel safe because the thief replaced the stolen item with a fake? With a copy, or even a random piece like the rhinestone bracelet Nick Perry had purchased that morning?

I wasn't sure how such a scheme would work, especially if the replacement didn't match what was taken. Given that I didn't have many other ideas at the moment, if I walked around this one and poked at it, it might start to take shape.

My first walk-around was that Lagarde, known for his excellent copies, had been mixed up in it. Maybe even unwittingly. Maybe something made him suspicious. At any rate, he had to be gotten out of the way.

With Lagarde dead, whoever was getting into the safe would need to find someone else to make copies. Hunting another reputable jeweler meant the risk of attracting attention. Which was why I pulled the DeSoto into a parking place down the street from a theatrical supply place.

"Hey, good-looking. Long time no see." The owner of the place straightened from the carton of greasepaint he was bending over and shot me a grin.

"How's tricks, Skip?"

"I could teach you a few if you're free for dinner."

"Your wife might object. Anyway, how do you know I couldn't teach you a few?"

He had a laugh that filled a room and a barrel chest to go with it. Today he sported red suspenders.

"Ah, Maggie. You break my heart every time you come through the door. Are you here to change how you look, or hunting gossip?"

I ducked a bevy of feather boas that hung from the ceiling.

"I'm here to avail myself of your wisdom."

On the other side of the velvet curtain behind him there was a snort. His wife, sewing sequins on a special order and chuckling, probably. I'd met them when a wealthy woman hired me to check the background of a young actor who was showing interest in her granddaughter.

"When someone around here needs a fancy necklace that looks like diamonds and such for a play or a girlie show, where can they buy that? Or get it made?"

Skip cocked his head and leaned on the display case in front of him. He eyed me shrewdly.

"Now that is a popular question today."

"Who else has been asking?"

"Not one of our regulars. Well-dressed gent. Came in right before noon.

"He claimed he was manager of a new show arriving in town. Told me one of their trunks had gone missing between here and Indianapolis, and he wanted to make sure they had the bijoux needed for a ballroom scene."

"He happened to mention which theater?"

"Nope."

"Name of the show?"

"Nope?"

"Give you a card or maybe an address where you could reach him?"

"No on both."

"Where did you send him?"

The shop owner stared at the case where his elbows rested. It held smoke pots, flash powders, spirit gum and a jumble of other things, all of it piled so densely only he, and maybe his wife, knew where to find things. When he lifted his head, concern had pressed lines in his face.

"I'll tell you, but the fellow I sent him to... I've only met him a time or two. He strikes me as shifty. Claims he doesn't make copies, just glues on chunks of colored glass he buys by the box like we do feathers and gloves and I don't know what all. I've never heard anything, except a house manager here and there grumbling he played fast and loose with his billing. But—"

"Thanks for warning me, Skip. I'll watch my step."

"His name's Rose. Delbert Rose."

He wrote down an address, which I tucked in my pocket.

"The man who came in asking before me, what did he look like?"

"Dark hair, mustache, medium build. Might have been downright handsome except for a couple of brown moles right above the bridge of his nose." He indicated one side.

It wasn't Perry. I thought a minute.

"Could the moles have been fake?"

Skip blinked, then nodded slow appreciation.

"Yeah. You'd think I'd pick up on something like that. The mustache, too. It wasn't the walrus type, but it wasn't a skimpy little Hitler type, either. Putty... spirit gum..."

As plain as the nose on your face, I thought. Or the moles, which would be the only thing people would remember about a man who wanted to change how he looked.

TWENTY-SEVEN

My immediate impulse was to pay a visit to Delbert Rose, who turned bits of colored glass into stage jewelry and was possibly shifty. Sticking with a plan I'd hatched earlier might yield more useful information, though.

I drove to the address I'd found in the phone book for the woman Nick Perry claimed was his great-aunt, or rather for her late husband. It was a big place, three stories of gray stone and more than twice the size of its neighbors. Stone gateposts anchored a black iron fence whose double gate stood open. Size, style and a mounting block to one side of the gate suggested it had been here long before its neighbors.

After leaving the theater shop, I'd used a pay phone to check on the recital the occupant of the house was supposed to be attending with Nick and Lena. It would last, I'd been told, at least another forty-five minutes, "followed by refreshments".

I hoped Great-aunt Clara had a sweet tooth, or at least a hankering for tea, but I couldn't count on it. Not after the way Lena had sulked at the whole outing. It seemed unlikely Nick or Lena would recognize my car, or even that they knew I had one. Still, no point taking chances. I parked the DeSoto on a side street, out of view of the Drake house, and walked to a house directly across from it.

A woman in a linen dress opened the door.

"Hello, I'm from Sterling Underwriters." I gestured with the clipboard, which held the form I'd gotten from Rachel, flashing it just enough for the woman to catch a peek at how official it looked. "I'm verifying information one of your neighbors supplied on his application for coverage. All quite standard, and of course confidential. Could you spare me a few minutes?"

"Insurance?" she frowned, trying to follow.

"Very similar, only for businesses when they start." I smiled.

"A neighbor, did you say?"

If anyone exists who isn't curious about the neighbors, I've never met them.

"Nicholas Perry. We understand he travels a great deal, but he's the nephew of Mrs. Clara Drake. He lists her address as his permanent residence."

"Oh, yes. The handsome young man who visits her every year or so."

It suggested she didn't really know their connection. That was fine.

"So he visits approximately every twelve months." I scribbled on a line that asked something about square footage. "And you've lived here how long?"

"Ten years--"

"Who else resides with Mrs. Drake? I see she's a widow."

"I don't believe anyone lives with her except her housekeeper. There's a girl who comes every day to clean."

"No children? Grandchildren?"

"I don't believe so. I don't really know Mrs. Drake, to tell you the truth. She doesn't mingle. Looks down her nose at the rest of us around here."

"So as far as you know, Mr. Perry is her only relative?"

I scribbled industriously.

"Yes. Well..."

I looked up.

"I'm not sure. She had a niece – grand-niece, more likely, now that I think of it. Sarah, I think it was. Very pleasant, always said hello. Then suddenly she wasn't around. I thought maybe she'd moved, or even died, but the girl who cleans for me talks to Mrs. Drake's girl, and she said Mrs. Drake had disowned her niece."

I asked if her household helper had gone home for the day, and if not, did she possibly know Sarah's last name or where she lived. The girl was still around, but she had no more to add.

"As I mentioned in the beginning, our interviews are confidential," I reminded the woman I'd spoken with. "We hope you'll keep that in mind and not mention my visit to Mrs. Drake or Mr. Perry."

I made a beeline to the house next door. It would shore up my story if she knew I'd talked to other neighbors besides her. It also might squeeze out more information about the cousin named Sarah. I glanced at my watch, aware of it ticking off minutes until Perry and his girlfriend returned with great-auntie.

The woman at the next house had a sprinkling of freckles that gave her a girlish look despite gray hair and glasses. She accepted my explanation of why I was there without question. She'd lived across from Mrs. Drake for going on thirty years, but only to say good-morning.

The only relatives she was aware of were Nick and Sarah. The little girl had grown up in Dayton. Nick's family had lived here at one time, but moved when he was fourteen or so. Sarah was a lovely young woman; used to accompany her great-aunt to a matinee or an afternoon of shopping.

"Married a man named O'Neill, I believe. Sam O'Neill. I read it in the paper. Last year I ran into her on the street. She was in a family way and absolutely glowing. I meant to knit a cap for the baby, but you know how it is. I asked where they were living, though, and she said on McClure."

When I asked why Sarah had stopped visiting Clara Duke, the knitter of baby caps merely shrugged.

"All I know is they had some sort of falling out."

TWENTY-EIGHT

Two more names to talk to now, one possibly crooked, the other a young mother, who by all indications was respectable. Unfortunately I didn't have time to talk to either until tomorrow. I had a blind date with a skinny bum named Punchy who might have seen goings-on in the alley behind the Canterbury, and might have been sober.

If I hustled, I could make a fast stop at the office, so I did. While skimming my mail I called Ab at Rike's to see if he'd picked up any scuttlebutt about Lagarde's murder. He rewarded me with two things I hadn't gotten from Boike. First, there'd been no attempt to get into the safe, or even the jewelry store itself. Second, the dead man's employees thought from things the police were checking that Lagarde had been killed as he left the store Friday night.

"They aren't open on Saturdays. Story is he always stayed late on Fridays and worked for a couple of hours. Toting up sales for the week, comparing to last week and month and year, checking inventory, then double-checking the whole shebang."

"A man for details."

"Sounds like it. Somewhere in there he'd usually telephone a cousin who's a jeweler in Phoenix or one of those places out there. Do a little horse trading sometimes, but mostly chew the fat on the company dime."

"Who'd you bribe to get information like that?"

"Doris, an old gal who's worked there forever. Her late husband and I worked together before I came here. She was putty in my hands once I asked her to lunch. A real pushover for our chicken salad."

"You're a devil, Ab. And a pal."

He laughed. I thanked him and set out to meet a bum called Punchy.

* * *

It was turning into a very long day, with a night shift still ahead of me. At a quarter till five, I backed the DeSoto into a parking space across from the soup kitchen Heebs had described, the one beside a church with a boarded up window. Less than two blocks away, where Fifth crossed Wayne Avenue, one of the nastiest parts of the city started its ooze. Once it got dark, I'd think twice, maybe three times, before coming here alone, even with my .38 handy. Now I sat and watched hungry people, most of them men and most with shoulders rounded by defeat, join the line forming at a place that would give them a hot meal.

It didn't take long for a wiry fellow I thought might be Punchy MacKenzie to make an appearance. He had his hands in his pockets and he kept checking the street. Either he was keeping an eye out in case he had to run for it, or he was looking for someone. The next time his head swiveled, I caught the glint of what might be a gold tooth.

Waiting for a trolley to pass, I crossed the street. A few of the men noticed me. Their looks were more sullen than anything else.

"You Punchy MacKenzie?" I asked.

"Maybe." Yep, he had a gold tooth, along with skittering eyes suggesting he might be sly or not-quite-right, or both. "You the one's gonna give me two-bits if I talk to you?"

I took a nearly new dollar bill from my pocket.

"I might give you this instead." I creased it lengthways so the snap would get his attention. "Depends."

He reached for the money. I moved it out of range. The line had advanced enough to leave a six-inch gap in front of Punchy. The man behind him tried to squeeze around into it. Punchy's arm swung out, hitting him hard in the neck.

"That's enough!" I thrust out my own arm, blocking the roundhouse the other man aimed at Punchy.

My sharpness, and maybe the deflected swing, made them both pause. I hooked a thumb at Punchy.

"Let's talk over there. I'll give you an extra quarter on top of the dollar if you lose a chance to get in here."

Punchy rubbed the back of his hand back and forth over his mouth. He nodded. We moved a few steps away to the curb. The man who'd taken Punchy's place was too pleased with himself to be curious.

"The alley behind Hotel Canterbury's your turf, I hear."

"Maybe." His eyes bounced. He looked at the dollar.

"That girl they found in the trash can back there, you see her?"

He shook his head vigorously.

"Alive, I mean. Her walking through the alley."

"Not alive or dead. You gonna give me the dollar?"

"You never look in the garbage cans?"

"Sure I do."

"Then how come you didn't see her body?"

Cunning gripped his sallow face.

"Have to time it just right to get there before the others. Good scraps out behind that hotel down the way. 'Bout half-past twelve I get there. Always head that direction soon as I hear those church chimes ring quarter past."

I wasn't following him and he knew it. He chortled at his own cleverness.

"No body to find when I went through back there on Wednesday. Thursday, I couldn't look in the can where they found her, now could I? Not with the night watchman at that place it belonged to sitting there playing cards with his pals till all hours like they do sometimes. Door open, they'd spot me for sure."

He stretched a hand out.

"You still owe me that dollar, though. I may not have seen anything, but I told you what I didn't see."

"Yeah. You did."

Moreover, it seemed to confirm Polly had been killed Wednesday, and sometime after twelve-thirty. I gave him the greenback.

"Not much Punchy misses." He tapped the side of his nose. "Men in that alley, coming and going. But no girls."

The soup kitchen opened its door. Cackling, he raced to the end of the line that was shuffling in.

The old guy was half crazy.

Which meant he was also half sane.

TWENTY-NINE

Since I was planning another late night, I thought it wise to fortify myself with dinner. As I approached the dining room, Lily-of-the-diamonds-Clarke stormed out with her husband hotfooting it after her as he attempted to get a word in.

"I *will* go home on Sunday, and you *will* take me someplace decent for dinner. Surely this wide spot in the road has one!" she snapped.

"But, Lily—"

"Why you had to come here in the first place is beyond me."

"Honey, I told you—"

"There's no one to talk to, nothing to do. Having brats in the dining room — in the *evening* — is the last straw!"

She drew up short, mainly because I was blocking her way. She started around me. I danced to the right. She moved the other way. So did I.

"Don't you think that little French boy and the Polish girl need to be with their parents after all they've been through?" I said, so mad I could spit.

Lily might be rich, but she wasn't smart enough to recognize I was blocking her way out of contrariness. We did our two-step again.

"What *they've* been through? Their parents chose to run. They let Paris fall to the Germans. Now *I'll* have to get my clothes from second-rate New York designers. And God only knows when we'll have decent champagne again. Get out of my way."

I did.

She stormed past with her husband still trying to pacify her. At the door to the dining room, Lena Shields had also turned to watch. Our gazes met in shared disgust.

"That takes the prize for selfish," I said, forgetting the role I was playing.

Lena didn't notice.

"That sow! She deserves every rotten thing that happens to her!" Behind her black-rimmed glasses her eyes fixed on the retreating couple as if unable to look away. "Pardon me," she said moving past me. "I've lost my appetite."

* * *

Shortly before midnight, I got up and put on an old tweed skirt and a sweater that had been darned on one arm. I laced up a pair of gum-soled shoes. They were ugly things not meant for anyplace but a gym, but they excelled at soaking up sound.

Tonight's schedule didn't call for talking to cleaning women in indoor comfort. Over the rest of the outfit I added a warm jacket. My .38 fit under it nicely. With a ham sandwich I'd ordered from Room Service prior to my shuteye stuffed in one pocket, I listened at the hall door long enough to be satisfied no one was coming or going. I eased the door open a sliver.

Click.

Had another door opened? Had one that had been ajar closed? I held my breath and tried not to pinch the small scrap of paper in my fingers. Two minutes passed. I counted the seconds. Finally, as silently as I could, I stepped out.

Alert for sound or movement in the hall, I slipped the scrap of paper between the latch and doorplate of my room. It muffled the faint scrape and snap of metal settling into metal. The door would stay closed and the paper itself wasn't likely to be noticed.

My steps were noiseless. I crept to the window at the end of the hall. I'd tested it when I returned from the soup kitchen. Now, as then, it glided up so silently I wondered if someone had oiled it. With a final glance back, I ducked through it onto the fire escape.

The metal gave a nearly inaudible chink as I dropped down. Stepping out of view, I pulled the window closed save for a crack large enough for my fingers.

Again I counted two minutes. If anyone had heard me leave, peddling a tale about stepping out for a breath of air would be easier to sell if I wasn't headed up the metal stairs to the floors above. When the time passed uneventfully, I did just that.

Shifting weight from foot to foot so the metal beneath me creaked as little as possible, I reached the third floor and ducked past a window identical to the one I'd climbed out. Driving through the alley a couple of times in daylight had allowed me to pick a spot on the fire escape that would give me the best vantage point. I could see not only the alley, but also the kitchen door to the hotel and the side street. Anyone coming down from the floor above would have to pass me, and I could move quickly if anyone sneaked out the window on this floor or the one below.

The only problem was sitting crosswise on one of the narrow stairs.

"Watch out for the boogeyman," a voice teased.

I tensed.

It was only someone leaving the kitchen. Seconds later a figure appeared, flapping a good-humored hand at whoever inside had spoken. Len the bartender, maybe? He turned down the side street.

Not much time passed before a clank at the far end of the alley caught my ear. Then another one, closer. A thin shape bobbed in and out of the edge of the shadows. Punchy making his rounds. It must be twelve-thirty.

He passed beneath me; found something good in the hotel garbage can, to judge by the smack of his lips closing over it; went on his way. More time passed. I ate the ham sandwich. I blew on my hands to keep my fingers limber. Soft as the rustle of leaves in a breeze, I heard the sound of a window sash easing open below me.

My hand slid to the Smith & Wesson. I peered through the metal grid of the step where I sat. An arm emerged from the window. A bundle the size of a tin can arced across the spindly rail of the fire escape and into the alley.

Seconds trickled in a steady stream. Finally, shadows across from the hotel and ten feet further along the alley shifted. A man's shape emerged, moving quickly. He darted across and bent to retrieve whatever had come out the window.

I'd planned for someone coming in or out, not a duo. While the man made his way to the street, I waited in vain for the sound of the sash below me closing. Only when the man with the bundle had turned out of sight did I hear the sash whisper down.

I breathed a time or two, then went down the stairs, sacrificing some of my previous stealth in the interest of speed. As I neared the window the bundle had gone out, I forced myself back to total caution. It was closed all the way now. The hall beyond it appeared deserted. I hurried past. I flew down the stairs to ground level.

Memory of the garrote across my throat was fresh enough for me to have the .38 in hand as I hit the alley. One quick sweep of the shadows for unfriendly shapes, and I took off for the street.

There. Half a block up. A man who walked with his elbows out. The man in the alley had walked with elbows out. Nice confirmation, though, since the street was otherwise empty. He stopped at the corner. Ducking into a bank entrance in case he looked back, I caught the sound of muffled steps behind me.

They stopped. Someone was following me. The person who minutes ago had tossed something out a window?

Fat white columns framed the front of the bank where I'd taken refuge. There was just space enough for me to squeeze between the nearest one and the front of the building. As the man behind me drew abreast of the column, I circled it like a carved horse on a small and dangerous merry-go-round. I came out behind my stalker, who held something between both hands. He turned into the entryway, expecting to find me. He had a fleeting second for puzzlement. Before he could look around, I yanked his arm double at the small of his back and slammed him face first against the side wall of the entry.

I shoved the Smith & Wesson against his head.

"Drop what you're holding and do as I say or you're dead."

I felt his reflex: Quick tensing, followed by pretended acquiescence. He meant to play along until he could jump me.

Something hit the ground by my feet. I was pretty sure I knew what it was.

"Lock your hands on top of your head. Spread your legs."

He resisted the second part, knowing it would slow his movements. I slid the tip of the gun to the back of his ear. He complied.

"Okay, Bartoz. How about telling me why you tried to kill me the other night in the alley?"

Up close I could see the cord securing his eye patch. He sneered, the sound of a man who didn't care whether he lived or died.

"It's what any Nazi-loving traitor deserves."

THIRTY

The accusation was so outlandish it threw me. Aware he was tensing to move, I ground the gun barrel into his head.

"What the hell are you talking about?"

Contempt permeated his whole being.

"All those measurements you write, with some tale about efficient workers. Watching. Timing. Is it the count you plan to assassinate, or is your President coming to this hotel while he's in town?"

Several things clicked into place. I stepped back cautiously.

"Bartoz, you've got it wrong. And whatever it is you and the count are up to, we're getting in each other's way. Keep your hands on your head and turn around slowly. Legs farther apart. Another step this way... and shoulders back against the wall."

I'd denied him the balance he needed for quick moves. His single eye blazed at me.

"Those measurements you found in my room don't matter a hill of beans. I'm working on something for the hotel. I needed a reason to wander around. FDR saved this country. He's got my vote any time he wants it. I don't know thing one about Count Szarenski, except if he's who he claims to be, he's some sort of war hero."

I'd lowered the Smith & Wesson. His eye flicked to it.

"Don't try," I said softly. It was aimed at his midsection. "Across from the hotel parking lot there's a luggage store.

There's a sign at the side of it that says *Chiropractor* with an arrow pointing down at some stairs. It's an after-hours place. You know what that is?"

"A bar. So what? You want us to drink together?"

"Yeah. I'll buy. I'll tell you exactly what it is I'm doing. What you tell me is up to you. Sorting this out might keep the two of us from working at cross-purposes."

He frowned. As good as his English was, my slang had thrown him.

"Keep us from getting in each other's way," I clarified.

Reading his expression was impossible.

"And if I don't?"

"After fifteen minutes, I call the police." I let my gun hand drop to my side. "Your choice."

With the toe of my shoe, I skimmed back the object he'd dropped. It was a garrote. I stuffed it into my pocket. Locking eyes with him, I turned my back and walked away.

It was a risk. I knew it. I'd taken one of his toys, but he could have a gun or a knife in his pocket. Dry mouthed, I kept walking. A display of nerve was the thing I thought most likely to work with someone like Bartoz.

* * *

The Chiropractor was faintly stuffy with a hint of dampness. Unable to crack a window, lest noise from its illegal trade draw attention, its only ventilation came from an open door into a storage room under the business upstairs.

I sat at a corner table, watching the door and sipping whiskey. Since I hadn't told Bartoz the password, I'd slipped the doorman a buck to let him in if he showed. Just as I was wondering what my next move should be if he didn't appear, he did. A few heads turned to look at him, then lost interest.

"So." He dropped into the chair across from me and lounged back with the confidence of a man who could hold his own in the roughest of dives. "You want to take me to bed? Where I come from, when a woman buys you a drink she wants to take you to bed."

"Don't flatter yourself. You're in America now."

He was trying to throw me, to gain the upper hand, but my gambit already had proved more effective than his. It had gotten him here and I hadn't taken a slug in my back.

The flesh-colored eye patch that didn't match his skin was, if possible, more unsettling up close than it was at a distance. On opposite sides of the patch, the ends of an angry red scar testified to the slash of a blade. Apart from the patch and the scar, he was good-looking. A chin that was firm without being defiant. A mouth that looked like it might have laughed before it was twisted by bitterness.

"How long have you worked for the count?" I asked, when he'd ordered whiskey too and the waiter had brought it.

"Two years. A lifetime. Why do you ask?"

"Just breaking the ice."

He considered it.

"Small talk."

"Yes." I crossed my arms on the table and leaned across them. "See I'm trying to figure out why you'd get such a crazy idea about me. Even considering the measurements."

His single eye stared at me without blinking.

"The reason I'm at the hotel, Bartoz, is that the owners think someone has gotten into the safe."

For the first time he looked startled. Interested even.

"Robbed, you mean?"

"They're not sure. Nothing appears to be missing. They hired me to investigate. They don't want me spooking the guests, so I'm pretending to be an efficiency expert."

His wariness, which I hadn't noticed was fading, returned full force.

"You are police?"

Shaking my head, I slid him the leather holder displaying the license that said Special Detective. He read it and thrust it back in a fury.

"Secret police!"

Tamping down frustration with him was becoming a challenge.

"No. 'Special' means private. A private detective. People hire me to find somebody who's missing, to see if a family member's stealing from their business. Things like that."

He considered a minute. He drank some whiskey as if he needed it.

"Then why are you sneaking around in the alley?"

"When someone goes out a back window – or in – they're usually up to no good. What are you doing back there?"

"Protecting the count."

"From what?"

"He has enemies."

"That's why you tried to kill me? That's why you killed that poor girl they found in the trash? To protect the count from enemies you won't even tell me about?"

He started so the dregs of his whiskey splashed to the rim.

"What girl? I haven't killed anyone!" His head lowered and he studied his hands for a minute. It made him look almost human. "Not in this country."

Bartoz drained his glass. I raised my hand and signaled the barman to bring him another. My own head I preferred to keep clear.

"I don't know anything about a dead girl," Bartoz said. "I go with the count and some men pick us up. They take us to another part of the city. They think he – the count – can muster support for Poland. Raise money for tanks and equipment since the United States seems content to see Europe bombed without lifting a finger."

"Raise money how? By selling expensive jewelry?"

He snorted mirthlessly.

"Women's play, back when the count and his friends were still in their homes. Donating bracelets and necklaces to buy bullets. Stripping them off at tea parties, dumping them into bags. So naive — all of us — imagining such efforts could buy enough rifles and ammunition to hold off the Germans for even a day."

The waiter delivered a full glass to him along with a murmured advisory. "Twenty minutes till closing."

Bartoz tilted the whiskey at me in acknowledgment. He sipped.

"The men he meets with organize gatherings," he said at length. "He speaks. They take a collection." He looked into the distance the same way I'd seen Mick Connelly do when longing for the country he'd left. "All as futile as the women back home donating their jewelry."

He tossed back half his refill.

"What's he looking for at the bank and the post office every morning?"

Caught off guard, Bartoz turned as snooty as a butler.

"That's not yours to know." He finished his drink. "We should leave. They close soon."

I rattled the ice in my glass to show him I had a few sips left. And was still the one with the upper hand.

THIRTY-ONE

Freeze wasn't pleased when I showed up in his office unannounced the next morning. I figured turn-about was fair play.

"Glad I caught you before your dance card for the day had you waltzing away," I said. "We need to have a chat about Polly Bunten."

The homicide lieutenant was in his shirtsleeves. I wouldn't have figured him for a loden green suspenders man. His elbows were propped on his desk as if they were the only things keeping him upright. It was the first time I'd seen him without a cigarette going. I felt a flicker of sympathy for him.

"Your client's off the hook," he said wearily. "The girl had a boyfriend. They quarreled. Next thing you know, she's dead and he's taken off, nobody knows where. We've bumped her case to the Unsolved file"

There was a chair in front of his desk. It seemed like a shame to waste it when he and Boike and two other detectives were the only ones in the room. I sat down.

"Anyone happen to mention the boyfriend left two weeks or more before she was murdered? There are witnesses."

"Witnesses," he repeated morosely.

I gave a quick recap. What Polly's acquaintances had told me. What I was really doing at The Canterbury. For reasons I couldn't explain, I skipped the parts about Count Szarenski and being attacked in the alley and Bartoz thinking I was a Nazi sympathizer.

"Let me get this straight," he said when I'd finished. "Nothing's been stolen out of the safe. But since there's jewelry in there and a jeweler's dead, you think this has something to do with Lagarde?"

Put that succinctly, it did sound far-fetched.

"And Polly Bunten. And the hotel guest buying thrift store jewelry. Look, Freeze, I didn't have to tell you any of this. The last thing my clients want is trouble, for their guests or for their business if word gets out about their safe. They thought it was right to let you know. So did I."

At last he scraped a match to life and started a cigarette. He took a drag. The haze of smoke between us reassured me I hadn't been talking to an imposter.

"You're a pain in the neck, you know that? Right about things just often enough I can't afford to toss you out on your ear without listening."

My percentage was better than that, but since he seemed to be getting soft on me, I didn't correct him.

"What I didn't hear—"

"Was anything that will stand up in court."

"Bingo. Look..." He pulled himself erect with effort. "In case you haven't heard, we've got the President of the United States coming to town. That means on top of the whole department already being short-handed, every cop in town now has meetings to go to, detective division has extra planning, all while I've got an uptown homicide I'm trying to solve. The Bunten case stays in the Unsolved file."

"Okay if I keep poking around them? As long as I bring you anything useful I turn up?"

He hesitated. The cigarette was between his teeth again.

"Yeah. Okay. But between you and me, that shrimp in the loud suits is crazy as a bedbug. He's probably imagining the whole business with the safe."

"He didn't imagine Polly's body."

Freeze didn't have a reply for that. I stood.

"Since you seem to think he made up the story about the missing man too, are you sure no bodies turned up around the time he reported that man missing from his hotel?"

Freeze glowered. Several seconds went by. He beckoned to Boike who trotted over with a file. Slapping it onto his desk, Freeze opened it and ran his finger down a page, flipped to another page and then another.

"Not unless the guest from the fancy hotel was a darkie who got a knife in his ribs for cheating in a crap game or a bum who ended it all in a flophouse down by the bus station."

"Anyone know the bum?"

"Nope. Drifter. Probably hopped off a freight."

"If I bat my eyelashes, any chance you'll give the flophouse address?"

Freeze once had claimed my detective work amounted to nothing more than batting my lashes to get information I wanted. It hadn't set well. The look he was giving me now indicated I'd worn out my welcome.

"If the missing man didn't exist, how about telling me what was in the envelope from the hotel safe?"

The smugness spreading over his face told me I'd stepped in it.

"Since you've been such a font of information, I guess it won't hurt to tell you. It was empty."

* * *

The encounter with Freeze had left a sour taste in my mouth. Returning to the hotel in my current humor probably wasn't the smartest thing I could do. It was still too early for the count and Bartoz to leave on their morning stroll anyway. If Nick Perry left, Smith would tell me which direction he'd gone. I went to my office and called Ab at Rike's, but he wasn't at his desk and he hadn't left any messages.

For the moment, I pushed aside questions I couldn't answer about the empty envelope and concentrated instead on Count Szarenski. What if I assumed he was waiting for some sort of deposit to his bank account, as opposed to being up to something fishy? If so, today he'd return to the same bank he'd visited yesterday. I found a small drugstore across from the bank but up the street and in the direction he would come from The Canterbury. Then I sat at the soda counter and sipped lukewarm coffee for fifteen minutes while keeping my eyes peeled on the route he'd followed the previous day.

I almost missed them.

It was the count's distinctive gait which caught my attention. They were coming at right angles to the way I'd expected, taking a different route. Caution on the part of Bartoz?

They went into the bank. They came out. As far as I could see, the count wasn't stuffing wads of money under his jacket. I expected the post office to be their next stop, and it was.

As on the previous day, the count came out with slumping shoulders. This time, though, they made another stop on their way back to the hotel. While Szarenski waited outside, leaning on his cane and looking dignified, Bartoz entered a small grocery store. A short time later he emerged with a bulging shopping bag in which I saw the round shapes of apples, or maybe pears, and what looked like a long loaf of bread.

Odd, carrying food back to a hotel overflowing with it, I thought. I went back to where I'd left my DeSoto, then circled a couple of blocks until I spotted the two men I was following. Driving slowly back to The Canterbury, I found a parking spot where I could watch.

They came back. They went in. I returned to my office and tried Ab again.

"Hey," he said. "I've been trying to reach you. One of the women who worked at Lagarde's came in and filled out a job application."

"Let me talk to her in your office and I won't charge for the background check."

"Or you'll rush one when I need it?"

"Deal."

"As it happens, one of the clerks in fine jewelry's retiring next month. We will have an opening to fill, so she won't be wasting her time coming."

"It wouldn't be Mona retiring, would it?"

"Sure would. Kind of surprised you remember her."

"Every time I walked by, she expected me to pinch something."

Ab laughed.

"Want to see if the Lagarde's lady is available this afternoon?"

"Three-thirty if you can swing it."

"I'll try. Call and check, though."

THIRTY-TWO

The sun was shining. The air had the crisp, dusty smell it gets in fall. It was a perfect morning to visit a man who made cheap fake jewelry. A man Skip thought was shady, possibly even dangerous.

"Delbert Rose?" I asked when he appeared from a back room.

He had an unpleasant mouth and eyes set too close together. He nodded across the counter separating us.

"At your service, sweetheart." He sounded so bored I wondered whether he ever slipped and used the line on men who walked in. "What do you need?"

"Oh..." I touched my hat and looked around as if overwhelmed by the place.

In contrast to the theatrical supply store's colorful jumble of items that teased with promises of enchantment to come, this place was drab. A mannequin to one side of the counter wore a jeweled headpiece guaranteed to strain the neck of the showgirl it adorned. From the neck down the same dummy wore a medieval frock with a belt of fake gemstones circling the waist. Wooden supply cabinets with drawers of assorted sizes lined a wall behind the counter.

"Well, you see, my employer's going out of town to a house party," I began. "She wants a copy made of a necklace. A friend recommended a jeweler, but he'd had a attack or something. Someone mentioned you—"

"I don't do copies, honey." He pointed to rods overflowing with flimsy metal shapes. "Three sizes of crowns, necklaces, bracelets, rings. Got plenty of chalices and swords. The costume person or whoever tells me what they have in mind. I show them what I've got in stock, tell them what else I could order. They pick the color of stones, maybe the size. That's all I do."

"But you could— Oh, jeez, this shoe is killing me." I tugged one off and kicked my leg up a little to massage my toes as his eyes followed. "You could match a *shape* though, right? Of a stone I mean."

"What? Sure. Maybe." He blinked and brought his attention back to what I was saying.

"I'll bet she'd say it was fine to just replace the ruby, this big, fat oval thing. The stones around it are just teensy little diamonds. They wouldn't matter much if something, um, you know, happened to it. Ordinarily, that wouldn't even cross her mind, but she doesn't know the people who invited her all that well. So since she really needs it, in kind of a hurry, could you replace just the ruby? Right in her necklace, but with one of your stones, I mean?"

I put my shoe back on and looked at him earnestly. He rubbed his lip.

"I'd have to look at it first."

"Oh, sure." I suspected he was weighing the odds. I put my thumb on the scale. "I guess maybe I should look at some of the glass ones like you'd put in. Make sure they're nice and all."

"Good idea, sweetheart."

Crossing to the supply cabinet, he pulled out a drawer and brought it over. Inside were glittering red stones of assorted shapes, all about an inch at their widest spot.

"I've got two larger sizes if these don't do."

I stared in fascination at the pretty fakes. As far as I knew, I'd never seen a real ruby, except maybe in some little oval earrings Rachel wore. In a nice setting the ones I was looking at would be enough to fool me.

THIRTY-THREE

It was on the early side for lunch, but I was hungry. When Jenkins got assigned to photograph some civic luncheon, as happened several times each week, he usually grabbed an early sandwich at the Arcade. I decided to go there in hopes I could kill two birds: appease my appetite and confer with my favorite nemesis.

Halfway through a crusty bun overflowing with cold pork, I saw his halo of red-gold curls bob in from the entry directly across from the Daily News building. With efficiency born of experience, he wound smoothly through the assortment of carts and stalls that filled the street level of the glass-domed rotunda. Two stops and he set course for the Third Street exit. His direction changed as he saw me.

"Hey, Mags." He dropped down next to me on a backless bench. "Shouldn't you be eating hummingbird under glass or something?" He popped a potato chip fresh from the fryer into his mouth. He transferred the paper cone holding them into his free hand, thereby gaining access to a frankfurter in the other.

"I worried I'd start putting on airs if I spent too much time with the international set. Is that film ready yet?"

"Jeez, Maggie. When did you start believing in miracles? It isn't something I can develop. Ione took it down to Cincinnati yesterday. On the train so she could carry it both ways."

"On the train?"

He nodded around a bite of frank. "Once she told me what was on it, I wasn't going to risk shipping it. With luck she'll be back today. I ought to bill you for what she'll spend shopping while she's there."

"She's sure worth looking at in what she buys, though."

He got the dreamy look he sometimes wore when he thought of her.

"Yeah. She is."

"Jenkins, is there any way to set up a camera so it would take a picture when somebody stepped in front of it?"

"Sure. Hire a fairy to flit down and press the release. Or maybe train a canary to land on it."

"I was hoping for sense here. There's no sort of gizmo you can attach?"

"Short of a string tied to the release that someone might or might not step on, no. Even that would jar the camera so you'd get a blurred image." He eyed me suspiciously. "Why?"

"Someone's been getting into my office. Pilfering my gin. I think it's the night watchman. I don't want to rearrange his ears until I have proof."

"Oh." Disappointed, he leaned over his camera and wolfed a few more bites. "Got to run. I take it you want to see that film when I get it back?"

"Yeah, I do."

I didn't expect it to show anything. The business with the movie camera had been mostly to bribe Jenkins into staying away from the hotel, with a dollop of authenticity for my role as efficiency expert as a bonus. Still, there was always an off chance that something on the film would give me an idea.

* * *

After Jenkins left, I spent another forty minutes or so sitting in the Arcade sorting out what I'd learned about goings on at the hotel. It added up to a lot and yet not much.

Who had dropped the bundle out of the hotel window last night?

Who was the man who'd retrieved it?

Why hadn't Bartoz, vigilant sentinel of the alley, followed him instead of me?

My failure to ask that particular question when I was sitting across from the man who could have answered it especially annoyed me. The accusation Bartoz had spit at me had rattled me more than I liked.

If I was going to roll in remorse, I might as well do it in the privacy of my office. As I neared the building, I noticed a big black Buick parked in front.

A man lounged lazily against the fender. He was thin and angular and even leaning against a car with his arms crossed, on a city street, he looked dangerous. Maybe more so on a city street.

"You get lost, Pearlie?" I asked in greeting.

"Rachel's getting her hair done. Sent me to try and find you. She wondered if you had time for a chat."

The first time we'd met, the two of them hadn't asked. They'd muscled me into a car with a gun in my ribs.

I consulted the watch pinned to my lapel. There was plenty of time before my meeting at Rike's, the status of which I still needed to check.

"I'm meeting someone at three." Better to have a half-hour cushion.

"This shouldn't take long. Rachel's got some kind of meeting downtown herself. And before that, foremen on two of her projects are coming in. Think she's going to read them the riot act."

His lips contracted in a grin reminiscent of a dog that flashed its teeth in warning. Pearlie took getting used to. He opened a door to the Buick and I slid into the back seat.

We only drove a couple of blocks before he pulled to the curb in front of a fancy salon whose windows were hidden by Austrian shades. Rachel marched out. She had on a russet suit that was right for the weather and possibly silk.

"Hair looks nice," I said as she got in beside me.

"The secret of my great strength. Like Samson." Satisfaction began to dance on her face. "My brothers were dumbstruck, and I do believe somewhat peeved, that their *shvester* had learned of Count Szarenski's arrival and they hadn't. Molière could have written another play if he'd seen the three of them and my father calling this acquaintance and that as they tried to get details."

"Which are?"

She smiled.

"Not a great deal more than what you told me. The count thought he had a cousin here and wanted to settle near family. But it looks as though he got the city wrong – maybe somewhere else in Ohio, maybe another city that starts with D."

"Detroit?"

She shrugged. "He's been meeting with some sort of Polish group, most of them born here, some who have been here for years. Working men, small business owners. They have a social hall north of the river, a block or so away from some church on Valley Street."

St. Adalbert, I thought.

Rachel lowered her window an inch. Her lighter snapped. We were heading east on Springfield. Houses mixed with factories, some still shuttered from when things went bust.

"These men the count meets with are raising money. Financing for some partisan group back in Poland." Her out blown smoke expressed her view of the scheme's futility. "They got wind of the count – or maybe he got wind of them. Anyway, he's become a big draw. He speaks at their gatherings. People cough up money."

It matched what Bartoz had told me last night.

"The group's beginning to put the word out to men who don't ordinarily come to their meetings," Rachel continued.

"Ones with fatter checkbooks, like my brothers. Joel, the lawyer brother, who actually sits down and talks to me sometimes as if I might have a brain, telephoned one of his friends. He barely got Szarenski's name out before the friend started telling how he was going to hear the count speak, and did Joel want to come."

"Are you going too?"

She snorted. "You think women are welcome?"

They had been at Irish meetings. Countess Markievicz, an Irishwoman married to a Pole, had plotted the 1916 Rising with Padraig Pearse and the others. When it failed, she'd berated the British for not having guts enough to execute her along with the rest of the leaders. Before and after her, hundreds of her countrywomen had asked questions and expressed opinions.

We turned onto the rutted street that led to Rachel's office. On my left was a coal yard. On the right was a fenced-in area where some sort of earth mover sat beside stacks of lumber and pipe. Pearlie stopped in front of the wooden building next door. A sign read MINSKY CONSTRUCTION.

"You've changed the last word," I observed.

"It describes the size of our projects better." Rachel slid through the door that Pearlie had jumped out to open. She leaned back in. "Joel's going to the meeting. I'll let you know if there's anything interesting."

"Thanks, Rachel."

"Do you still want me to try my questionable language skills with the count and his wife? To ask questions on your behalf?"

"If you're willing."

"No guarantees he'll even see us."

"I know. Any chance you could make it tomorrow?"

"Four o'clock."

Rachel closed the door briskly. With her decisive stride, she marched toward the building that was her office and her pride. Pearlie resumed his spot under the wheel.

"Okay if I move up front?"

"Makes me nervous." He put the Dodge into gear and we pulled away. I gathered he was taking me back to my office.

"Are you still taking piano lessons?" I asked.

I caught the flash of his teeth in the rearview mirror. His nickname, I assumed, derived from their whiteness.

"Just started working on a Jelly Roll Morton piece. Told my teacher I'd quit if she gave me any more minuets."

I was surprised his teacher knew any Jelly Roll Morton. I tried to picture him playing a minuet.

The drive from Rachel's office to downtown took less than ten minutes. I waited until we were almost there to raise a question that had been on my mind.

"Pearlie, I hope it won't damage your opinion of me if I tell you my work had caused me to be acquainted with some unsavory characters."

"Unsavory." He rolled the word around on his tongue. Pearlie liked to enhance his vocabulary. "Rats, you mean?"

"Small ones. The sort who tell me things for a price."

"Because they know you won't squeal."

"Or because I know things about them that could make life unpleasant for them if they don't. Now, though, I need information I don't think any of them can provide. I'm hoping you might know someone who can."

"Maybe." His eyes met mine in the mirror. He gave his canine smile. "I know one or two unsavory people, too. What sort of information?"

I scooted forward and rested my chin on the back of the seat.

"Who around here fences expensive jewelry? The sort the Kettering-Patterson crowd might wear?"

He nodded serenely, maybe thinking about minuets.

"My guess, nobody local could handle something like that," he said finally. "You're talking Cincinnati, Cleveland, maybe Detroit."

THIRTY-FOUR

Melva Cummings was middle aged, nicely groomed, and looked as if she hadn't slept well for several days.

"I like the place I'm working now." Her voice wobbled slightly. "I've been there twelve years. But Mr. Lagarde didn't have any family. When things settle down, I expect the store will be closed." She frowned. "Does that seem callous? Thinking ahead like that?"

"Not a bit."

We sat on opposite sides of a desk in a tiny room adjoining Ab's office. Ab used it for grilling shoplifting suspects and conferring with department managers on confidential matters. I'd already asked Melva all the things I covered on a background check, which I didn't usually conduct in person. I was edging into questions for my own purposes.

"I suppose I'd be less than honest if I didn't admit I'm nervous working there now as well," she said. "I'm not a fraidy-cat, but every time the back door opens..."

She looked down at her hands. They were clasped on top of the navy blue cotton gloves she'd removed when she sat.

"It shakes you when something like that happens," I reassured. "Especially if you're the one who found him."

"Oh, no, I didn't. Mercy! But I did... I did hear him arguing with a man Friday morning. From all their questions

– the police – I'm sure they think it could have been the man who killed him." She shivered involuntarily.

My ears had grown as long as Peter Rabbit's.

"Goodness!" My brain scrambled after innocent-sounding questions that would wring out what she knew. "Was he someone who'd been in the store? A regular customer?"

Her head shook once. "I'd never seen him before."

She seemed willing enough to talk. Glad to, perhaps, when she wasn't sitting across from someone with the authority of a policeman. Maybe she didn't have a girlfriend or female relative to whom she could spill out worries. I put my fountain pen aside.

"I've always wondered, do robbers and, well, killers, do they look like the faces on those Wanted posters down at the Post Office?" I hunched over my folded arms. "Mean, I mean. Did he?"

We were talking woman-to-woman now. Melva warmed to it.

"Oh, I just caught a glimpse, really. It was first thing. Mr. Lagarde must have just opened up. I came in the back way like we always do and was hanging my hat up when I heard someone shouting – angry. Well, I thought... I'm not sure what. That I should see if there was trouble, I guess."

Melva, as she'd claimed, was no fraidy-cat.

"So I peeked through the door to the front of the store, and saw a man snatching up an envelope Mr. Lagarde had given him — Are you sure you want to hear all this?"

I nodded. "I'm curious what he looked like, of course. You know, if he looked like the posters? But some of these details may interest Mr. Simms. There might be something he'd think it prudent to caution the clerks here to be alert for."

Her eyes widened.

"You were saying something about an envelope?"

"Oh. Yes. It was one of the thick manila ones like we put jewelry in when someone brings it for repair or appraisal. I didn't catch what the man said, but Mr. Lagarde apologized, told him something was excellent quality. The man stormed out, and I heard the other clerk and our assistant coming in the back way, and that was that."

"And what did he look like? In that little glimpse?"

"Not hard like the faces on the posters. In fact, I remember thinking that if he hadn't been so furious, he might have been quite good looking. Well, except for two moles right here, next to his eyebrow."

* * *

In the interest of fairness, I tried on several explanations after I left Rike's. Only one of them fit like a glove.

An unknown customer had quarreled with Lagarde shortly before I saw Nick Perry return to the hotel in a fury. Perry had refused to answer his girlfriend's question about where he'd been. He'd used a disguise he could put on in a minute or less in a public restroom, or even using the reflection from a shop window. One he could discard as easily.

Perry was the man with the moles that drew attention away from all other details about him. The one who'd visited Skip hunting someone to make copies of jewelry. The one Melva had overheard arguing.

And probably the one who'd killed Polly and Lagarde.

Walking back to my office, I looked at other aspects of my theory. The man who'd quarreled with Lagarde had left jewelry. If the man was Perry, then the jewelry had come from The Canterbury's safe. So that, too, made sense. But what had caused the quarrel?

According to Melva, Lagarde had told his visitor something was excellent quality. His own workmanship? Maybe. He might have been apologizing because the work his visitor wanted would require too much time. Or suppose... suppose the jewelry he'd been asked to copy had, on closer inspection, turned out to be a high quality fake?

Like the stone in Mrs. Szarenski's necklace that Daniel Drew, the jeweler who'd evaluated every piece in the safe, wasn't sure about.

"Yes!" I said, jabbing the elevator button and practically dancing as the ancient cage shimmied and shuddered up to my floor. "Yes, yes, yes!"

That scenario answered the question about why Perry hadn't simply cleaned out the safe and run. Sneak something out. Get a copy made. Return the copy to the safe while you sell the real thing for tens of thousands of dollars, maybe more. If you had the nerve to pull it off, chances of having it noticed were almost nil. You faced none of the risk of an out-and-out burglary.

If Perry had concocted a scheme that clever, risked getting into the safe, and then discovered what he'd stolen was only a fake, he'd be furious. Especially if he'd been noticed by an unfortunate cleaning girl whom he'd killed to silence.

The elevator stopped. I waved at Maxine and her daughter-in-law through the glass front of Simpson's Socks wholesaler as I passed. Maxine wasn't in black today, and I didn't see the sign she'd been carrying. By the time I opened the door to my office, however, my good mood was waning. As neatly as the various puzzle pieces fit when I'd worked them out downstairs, I still lacked proof.

Okay, I'd dig in and get some. I could follow Nick Perry tomorrow and see where he went. Or I could sit and observe who called on Delbert Rose, who claimed his only business was sticking chunks of colored glass on cheap tin crowns and such. If I was on the right track, I'd bet the two crossed paths at some point.

I wanted to find out more about Rose. Also, although I couldn't see how it fitted with any of this, I wanted to find out more about the stiff in a flophouse Freeze had mentioned. As unlikely as that connection seemed, I couldn't let go of the fact his body had turned up not long after an unknown man went missing from The Canterbury.

The vanished guest had left something in the safe. Someone — I was going to say Nick Perry — was getting into the safe.

A trip to Finn's might help me see things more clearly.

THIRTY-FIVE

Wee Willie had walked his mail route fighting a cold and reeking of camphor. He'd only ordered half a pint and was nearly through with it when I came in. He looked so miserable I didn't have the heart to torment him.

"It's how the devil punishes us for kissing girls," he said hoarsely.

"Those little devils you call kids aren't punishment enough for kissing your wife?"

"Not me. Our oldest smooched some little girl on the playground last week. Next day she started sneezing. Then he did. Now me."

"That's about how I remember you courting Maire. The smooching part anyhow."

Willie caught a sneeze in a well-used handkerchief and made an inelegant exit. I took my nearly full glass to a table. Time to think through my theory about Nick Perry again. The more I did, the more my mood deflated. With a little work and anything short of lousy luck I'd be able to link him to thefts from the hotel safe. What I couldn't see was any way to prove he was Polly Bunten's killer.

She'd been young, and poor and struggling to provide for a kid. By society's standards, she hadn't counted for much. There were thousands like her. But she was a human being. She deserved to have someone held accountable for her murder.

"You look as glum as I was last time you were here."

It was Connelly. How had I failed to detect his presence when he stood right by my table?

"Just lost in a case." I looked past him. "Seamus isn't with you?"

Usually Seamus came in with Billy. Sometimes, though, he and Connelly came in together. Often that meant Seamus had a new phonograph record, some piper or fiddler or whistle player, which he and Connelly were heading off to listen to after their pints.

"He and Billy were bound for a meeting at the Hibernians."

"The Hibernians!"

Chuckling, he dropped into the chair across from me.

"What's wrong with that?"

"Nothing. It's just... Billy and Seamus?"

What was wrong was getting hit in the face with the fact two men I loved and thought I knew belonged to a group that possibly wasn't so different from the one attended by Count Szarenski and Bartoz. Except, of course, that one was Irish and one was Polish.

Connelly was frowning.

"Maggie, it's only a club. Your dad belonged too. It's not like they're smuggling rifles. They're raising funds for some fellow who needs an operation."

"Yeah, forget it. Like I told you, I've got a tough case." I drank some Guinness, stinging from the additional discovery that he knew something about my father which I hadn't. Connelly was prudent enough to let me be. He savored his pint. Finally I slid him a look. "Do you belong, Connelly?"

He tilted back his head. His Adam's apple quivered with quiet laughter, which made me bristle.

"Would it matter one whit what I answered?"

"No."

"Well, then." Sitting upright, he fixed me with piercing blue eyes. "The answer is No. But someday I might change my mind. Now finish your Guinney and meet me at that place on Fifth in half an hour. We'll have some supper and you can tell me about this case that's got you in knots."

* * *

The place on Fifth had been there forever. Its age showed in brick walls supporting high ceilings. A long bar stretched the length of the room where you entered. A doorway to the right led into a good-sized dining room with scarred plank floors.

Connelly had gotten there first. He'd gone home to change into slacks, shirt and vest. We sat by one of the windows opening onto the street. It was cracked to let in a breath of fall air.

"Now," he said when we'd ordered. "You going to tell me how you really came by this?"

Before I could react, he reached across to push down the silk scarf I wore and trace a finger down the pencil-line scab on my throat. I shoved his hand away, but not in time to stop a spurt of heat.

"I already told you. A tree branch hit me."

"I'm a country boy, remember? Tree branches don't cut like that. Garrotes do."

His voice had hardened. My breath slowed.

"And no, I don't know that because I've used one, if you're wondering." He looked away briefly.

Connelly had done things during his life in Ireland. Things that went with seeing family members killed for their politics. Things that wouldn't be understood here.

"Yeah, that's what it was," I admitted. "You don't need to gloat, though."

He managed the ghost of a smile as his brief tension eased.

"And here Billy's pleased as punch you're safe working at some fancy hotel."

I laughed.

"Now tell me what led to it, and how you managed to get clear. There's not many who escape one of those."

His patient concern filled me with guilt. Here he was, concerned about me. And here I sat, too much of a coward to make the short trip for my father's pipes so I could give them to the one man worthy of them. The man who, if I were a different person, I might settle down with.

"I'd rather hear about Chicago. Tell me you had at least a little fun out of it."

"Heard some grand music anyway. Mad as I was, I knew I'd never sleep, so I stayed up all night, going place to place with a couple of fellows I met. Ended up in the back of one that had closed, listening to two fiddlers try and outdo each other. I slept all the way back on the train."

"Now, quit trying to wiggle out of it and tell me about this case that's troubling you."

So, as other tables filled with diners and we settled into our meal, I did. I described the goings on at the hotel, the attack in the alley, and last night's bizarre set-to with Bartoz.

"This fellow with the eye patch sounds like a bad one to tangle with," he said when I'd finished.

"No argument there."

"Can't see any reason he'd get mixed up in stealing jewelry, though. I'd say you're on the right track with Perry."

I stared.

"Are you saying you believe Bartoz was prepared to kill because Count Szarenski really *does* have enemies?"

Connelly studied his coffee cup.

"I'm saying Bartoz believes he does. Where they've just come from, it was probably true."

My eyes fell closed in frustration.

"It makes sense to him, Maggie."

"Yes. I understand."

Connelly's father and brother had both been victims of Ireland's political woes. He could see things from Bartoz's view.

I shoved aside my plate with its last bite of Salisbury steak and spoonful of peas. A truth I'd been avoiding breathed in my face. All I knew was one city and one way of life. How could I begin to guess whether someone whose whole experience and culture had been different from mine did something out of guilt or innocence? How could I predict what they might do?

"I read the papers every day," I said in frustration. "France and Dunkirk and now bombs falling in London. I thought I knew plenty about what's going on over there, but the fact is it's been no more real to me than a Pearl Buck story or a cowboy movie."

I nodded thanks to the waiter who was clearing our plates. Resting my hands on the table, I toyed with a stray crumb while Connelly listened in silence.

"Every last person who could shed light on the safe business or Polly's murder either came from over there or lived there for months at a time. They've sat in places and walked in streets I've only read about. They see things differently. Like you did with Bartoz."

"I lived in a mud street Irish village. You know as much about London as I do.

"What I do know is, much as I've hated England, it's now the only thing standing between the Nazis and Ireland. If America doesn't send help, my ma and the kids could soon have worse than Unionists or Black and Tans breaking their door down — while I sit over here twiddling my thumbs. You think that doesn't feel like make-believe? You're making too much of this, Maggie *mavourneen*."

"Oh, *am* I?"

"People and the reasons they do things aren't that different, no matter where they come from. If Perry's your man, like as not he's stealing out of simple greed, same as any other crook."

"And if he's not? I can't trust my instincts on this one, Connelly. I can't rely on things I've learned in the course of my work all these years."

"You're a smart woman, Maggie, regardless you've traveled or not. You're good at your work. More than good. Stop trying to sell yourself short."

His hands covered mine and squeezed gently.

It felt too comforting to pull away.

THIRTY-SIX

It was going on ten by the time I got back to The Canterbury. Connelly and I had lingered over pie and coffee, then walked along the river. Sometimes we'd talked, but much of the time had been spent in comfortable silence. The autumn night was so still we could hear the rush of the water. Stars spangled the surface. It had been a long time since I enjoyed that kind of evening.

The hotel lobby felt stuffy by contrast. A handful of men stood at the bar in the lounge. Bartoz sat in his usual spot facing the door. I'd never noticed him there after dinner. At sight of me, his chin lifted.

It might have been acknowledgment. It might have been a summons. The answer came as I continued toward the stairs. He rose at once to join me.

"You could have informed the police about me. You didn't. You could have caused the count trouble. You didn't. I think there is something useful I must do for you." His words were hurried. "The man you were following last night, the one you lost because of me, I know where he'll be soon. He meets with a hotel guest."

"Perry?"

He looked startled. "Yes."

"How do you know?"

"I've watched them. Twice. Always the evening after Perry throws a package from the window. Always about this time. They meet in a bar. I can show you, but we must hurry. Perry went out minutes before you came in."

I'd been set up often enough to know he could be baiting a trap.

"What street?"

Bartoz shook his head. "I don't know street names. That way." He gestured.

I made a show of looking at the clock behind the reception desk.

"My cousin's ready to have a baby any minute. Just let me check to see if she's gone to the hospital."

It was the sort of thing a man wasn't likely to question. Using a house phone while Bartoz watched from a distance, I dialed Tucker's private number.

"I'm going out with Bartoz," I said when Frances answered. "If I'm not back by midnight, call the number I give you and tell the woman who answers who I left with."

Rachel would still be up. She'd call Pearlie. The two of them would move faster and more effectively than the police. Unless she was out, in which case I'd be up a creek.

I walked back toward the man with the eye patch. Uneasiness tugged at my gut. By not going upstairs, I'd sacrificed the chance to tuck my Smith & Wesson into my purse, but I kept my .22 automatic under the DeSoto's passenger seat. All I had to do was reach my car a few steps ahead of Bartoz and transfer it to the door pocket.

"If we take my car we can catch up, maybe even get there before him," I said as we stepped out into the night.

Bartoz nodded. If he'd said we could walk, I'd have faced a hard decision. I'd put odds I could trust him at two-to-one. It was covering the one that might keep me alive.

As we neared the DeSoto, I hurried ahead.

"Got to clear some things out of the seat," I called over my shoulder.

With one hand I picked up the clipboard and magazine I kept on the passenger side. With the other I slid the automatic from under the seat. Its reassuring angles disappeared into the door pocket next to me just as Bartoz opened the door on the opposite side. I pitched the other items into the back.

"Nice car," observed Bartoz as I turned the key. It was the closest he'd come to social niceties.

"Reliable, too. Which way?"

He pointed south.

"After some railroad tracks you'll turn east."

Was he testing my nerve? He was routing me past my own office.

"Why did you follow Perry the first time? Did you think he was plotting to harm the count?"

"I heard movement in the hall one night. Very late and very quiet — a bad combination. I watched and saw someone throw something out. Perry. When he returned to his room, I went down the back way. There was a man in the street moving... not like a bum. Leaving. Accomplishing something.

"Turn here."

It was warm enough that our windows were down. Bartoz lighted a cigarette.

"The group that I told you about had approached the count about speaking. I wasn't sure what game Perry played. I've kept my eye on him." He flicked some ashes off. "An apt expression in my case, don't you think?"

If he was making it up, he spun as good a tale as I did.

"Twice before now, I've seen him leave without the woman. Late, but not too late. Like this. There's a way a man moves when he wants to get somewhere without attracting attention."

"The way he carries his shoulders."

"Yes. Naturally, I followed. He came here, where we're going. Turn."

We were south of where I'd had supper with Connelly. The area was a mixture, homes and mid-sized businesses. Things were run-down here, but not as disreputable as they became closer to Wayne.

"Tell me about the Frenchwoman."

"Frenchwoman? Ah, you mean Madame Houdin. She's American, though she's lived away long enough to be mistaken for French. Her husband's family was very old, with extensive lands.

"He was a painter. One of some reputation. The count had one of Houdin's works in his grand salon. After Paris fell, Houdin joined a partisan group. He was killed. She fled to keep the boy safe, I assume."

His intact left eye slid toward me. If he was playing a game tonight, part of his brain would now be occupied wondering why I'd asked.

At his direction I made a few more turns and parked across from the sort of bar which drew clerks and shop owners rather than workingmen. It would be a good place for meeting without being noticed.

If Perry had come here. If Bartoz wasn't inventing it all. He finished his cigarette and lighted another.

"You told me you were in the alley the night you attacked me because you were protecting the count. Going to one of the meetings across the river. What you didn't explain, is why he goes out the back way."

The man beside me was silent so long I started to suspect he was having trouble fabricating an answer. When he finally spoke, however, his voice sagged with the weariness of truth.

"He doesn't want anyone to know the women are unprotected."

"In a good hotel? With locks on the doors and people around?"

"When he was away fighting, near the end, the Germans came to his house in the country. Only a few peasants — farm workers — and some elderly servants were there to defend it. They were slaughtered. Some German officers broke down the door. They raped the count's sister. They were trying to do the same to his wife. Julitta shot one. I was in the attic, delirious with fever from my wounds. They tell me I crawled down and shot the other."

A man came out of the bar we were watching. It was Perry. He paused where light from inside caught his face. He touched the breast of his jacket.

"He's got something under there," I said. Wrong place for a gun. "Did he have it when he left the hotel?"

"No. The man he meets gives him something. The first time I followed, there was a truck parked in front. It made nice camouflage for me to go closer and watch. I saw."

"Any idea what it is the man gives him?"

"Money, perhaps? I think Mr. Perry is stealing things from the hotel. From the rooms." His tone was disinterested.

Perry tosses something out a hotel window.... An accomplice retrieves it.... A night or two later, Perry meets a man in a bar and the man gives him something. According to Bartoz, both parts have happened more than once. And in the daytime, someone who might be Perry wearing phony moles and a phony mustache asks about getting quick copies of jewelry.

Could Perry be coming here to pick up copies and stroll nonchalantly into The Canterbury with them tucked into his pocket?

Maybe. It might just make sense.

"You're not worried he might harm the count?"

Bartoz sneered.

"I was. I watched. Perry is a thief and a leech who lives off women, nothing more."

The man we were talking about looked around. He started to walk.

"Does he go back to the hotel when he leaves here?" I asked quickly.

"Yes."

"Directly?"

"Yes."

"And the other man?"

"Has a car."

Meaning Bartoz had no idea where he went. Even as I tried to decide my next move, another man emerged from the bar. Bartoz touched my arm.

"There. Him."

The man turned in a different direction than Perry. He walked with his elbows out like the man from the alley.

"I want to see where he goes. You can go on back, see if Perry turns up. A trolley will stop at that sign there in a couple of minutes. It runs right past the hotel."

"The man who came out, if he deals in stolen goods, could be dangerous. I'll come too."

"Thanks, but I can manage."

"You'll lose him if you argue. Go."

THIRTY-SEVEN

The thought of the automatic in the door pocket at my side reassured me. My aim with my left hand wasn't as good as with my right, but it was still better than average. When the unknown man got into a car and started away, I followed. Mostly I hung back half a block, varying it at intersections or when the occasional car intervened.

"You follow well," Bartoz observed as we made our way back across town.

I welcomed neither his assessment nor his assumption I needed one.

"What time is it?" I asked tersely.

He showed me his wristwatch. An hour and a half remained before Frances sent out the troops. It surprised me how little time had elapsed.

"I don't think I've been in this part of your city before. When the count gives a speech, some men pick us up near the hotel. They drive, but a different direction."

"You go north. Across the river."

"How do you know this?" He'd grown wary.

"That's the Polish neighborhood. Over by St. Adelbert's church."

He fell silent. My purse rode along on the seat between us. His eye moved toward it, maybe speculating that my .38 was inside and out of my reach.

"You're not afraid of me," he said as I downshifted at an intersection.

"I'd be a fool not to be afraid of you, Bartoz."

"Yet you came tonight."

"I do what I need to for my job."

"Yes. I also."

The car I was following was a Chevrolet, gray as nearly as I could make out in the dark, and with plenty of years on it. It turned into a neighborhood between Warren and Patterson. Things were several steps better than where Polly Bunten had lived, but the area was nonetheless shabby.

The Chevy stopped in front of a three-story house. A sign in a front yard the size of a table advertised ROOMS. The man who'd met with Perry got out of his car and retrieved a duffle bag of what looked like laundry. Whistling softly, he let himself into the darkened rooming house.

"Stop here and watch," whispered Bartoz. "I'll walk to the corner where I can see the other side. If I start back this way, drive to the corner and wait for me. If not, pick me up there in five minutes."

He was out before I could speak, nudging the car door so it closed with a muted click, then vanishing into the shadows. He was good at fast planning, I'd give him that. My heart hammered. The house between me and the rooming house had a light on in a back room. Otherwise, the street was dark.

My hand closed on the automatic and transferred it to my right hand. I couldn't see Bartoz at all. I pushed the lock down on my door and cranked the window up. I couldn't reach the locks on the rear doors at all, and sliding across to the one on the passenger side would make me vulnerable. The rooming house remained dark.

Then, at the end of the block, a figure stepped into the street and started toward me. I wasn't sure it was Bartoz. As it came closer, though, the chin raised as his had when he'd signaled to me at the hotel.

Leaving my lights off, I started the engine. As the car crept forward, the figure ahead veered suddenly to the side with the rooming house and disappeared again. What the devil?

I drove to the corner and switched my lights on low. In my rearview mirror I could see a light in a third floor window. Had five minutes passed? Was I crazy, sitting here waiting for Bartoz when I wasn't sure if I trusted him?

Nothing moved on the street. Nothing I could see. The door across from me flew open. I swung toward it, leveling the automatic.

"Don't."

It was Bartoz.

"I ought to. You scared the peewadding out of me."

I leaned back and tried to summon saliva. Bartoz slid in next to me and closed the door almost without a sound.

"The light went on shortly after I stopped to watch. It's his room, I think. I went into the vestibule thinking there might be postal slots, something with names."

"And?" I changed gears and let out the clutch.

"There was some sort of rack, with things written. But there was no light, and I didn't have a torch."

THIRTY-EIGHT

"Good morning, sunshine." Connelly's cheer spilled into my unwilling ear through the phone that had wakened me from a sound sleep. "I have an address for you if you'd like to come get it."

"Are you nuts, Connelly? I'm still in bed."

"Ah, I'd better come up then."

I shot upright, fully awake.

"You're in the lobby? Please tell me you're not in uniform."

"Pressed and shined with cudgel at the ready. Not in the lobby, though, more's the pity. I'll bet you're a treat with your hair tangling over a pillow."

My blood surged harder than it had when Bartoz yanked my car door open the previous night.

"What did you say about an address?"

"The one you mentioned you hadn't been able to find."

The flophouse with the unidentified body? It had to be. I hadn't asked him to find it, though. Since Freeze had refused to give it to me, I'd avoided involving Connelly.

"Have you something to write it down with?" he asked patiently.

I reached for the pencil and paper on the nightstand.

"Thanks, Connelly. I didn't expect this," I said when I'd finished.

"I know. It worried me, you being so down in the dumps you didn't try some trick to get me to help. Look,

Billy let me out at a pay phone and I see him coming to pick me up. Keep safe."

* * *

My first stop of the day was in a pleasant neighborhood at a cottage not much larger than a playhouse. One cheek of the moderately pretty young woman who opened the door looked flushed and sweaty. The other side of her face was fine. The infant whimpering on her hip as she opened the door possibly explained the dichotomy.

"Mrs. O'Neill?" I asked with a smile.

"Yes?" She shushed the baby on her hip, looking distracted.

"My name is Maggie Sullivan. I'm a private detective. I'd like to ask you some questions about your cousin. Nick Perry."

Both sides of her face grew equally granite-like.

"I haven't seen my cousin for twelve years or more. I don't know where he is or anything else about him. Try our great-aunt, Mrs. Carlton Drake."

She started to close the door. I leaned my shoulder against it.

"I know where he is. He's right here in Dayton. And thick as he is with your aunt, I doubt she'd give me the sort of information I need."

Part of the hostility in her eyes gave way to interest. Then her kid progressed from whimpering to full-blown fuss. Tears started to spill and he tugged at his ear.

"I don't know anything that would help. Excuse me. I have a sick baby."

"Then I better come in, hadn't I? So he's not in a draft."

I knew she wouldn't risk bumping the kid if we tussled over the door. A second passed, then she stepped aside.

"Really, I really don't know what I could— There, there, baby, Mama knows it hurts."

"It is a boy, right?" I'd made a stab in the dark.

She nodded wearily. "He has an earache. Shh, shh, there now." The baby, who didn't look quite big enough to walk, pressed his head to her cheek.

Inside and out, the house I'd entered was neat as a pin, with white walls and lace curtains. It was also tiny, probably just this front room plus a kitchen and bath and bedroom in back. Quite a change from her Aunt Clara's big place and her cousin's high living. The neighborhood was good, though.

"You didn't seem surprised when I told you I was a detective."

"Not when you mentioned Nick in the same sentence. Except for your being a woman, of course. Nick's parents gave him everything. Our aunt and uncle – great-aunt and uncle, really – adored him. Yet ever since we were children he's been a bad apple. Not just boyish pranks, *bad*." She glanced briefly up from the baby. "You're not here because you're trying to help him, are you?"

"No."

"Good."

She hadn't asked me to sit. I didn't, even as she settled herself in an armchair and eased what I knew by the shape was a hot water bottle wrapped in flannel between her cheek and the baby's ear.

"I honestly don't know much about him. He's five years older. We saw each other at family gatherings, parties by our parents' friends. That was the extent.

"They moved away, his family did, when I was nine or ten. They came back summers to visit. The last time they came, Nick... stole something." She swallowed. "From a friend of Uncle Carlton's....

"Please don't ask my husband's family about it. Aunt Clara is the only relative I have left, and she wants nothing to do with me since I married a Catholic. My in-laws know she disowned me, of course, but not about—"

"I didn't intend to."

"It never even occurred to me to mention Nick, let alone —"

"What did Nick steal?"

Sarah started to shake her head, but remembering the baby, turned one palm up instead.

"I don't know. My parents whispered. I think Uncle Carlton made things right with the other man, but even young as I was I could see my uncle was heartbroken afterwards. The idea someone related to him would do such a thing, I suppose."

"What was the other man's name?"

"I'm not sure. Russell? But that could have been his first name. He had bad lungs. They moved to Arizona or one of those dry places. I think it might have been around the time that Uncle Carlton died."

She eased herself to the edge of her chair, preparing to stand. The baby whimpered.

"He has a doctor's appointment. If you'll excuse me..."

"I'll let myself out so you don't have to jostle him more than necessary. And thanks." I took a step, then paused. "It must be tough, being estranged from your aunt after all you did for her."

"Actually, it's a relief. She's a very difficult person. I don't believe she appreciated a thing I did for her."

To reassure the frazzled young woman she'd be rid of me, I waited until I was at the door to speak again.

"What about Nick's friends? Are any of them still around?"

"I don't even know what school he attended. When we were at Aunt Clara's he'd sneak off sometimes with the son of a chauffeur or gardener or something who worked in the neighborhood. But as far as actual friends, I've no idea."

THIRTY-NINE

Mothers with young kids got into gear early because they had to. It was why I'd put Sarah O'Neill at the top of my places to go that morning. In contrast, I'd expected someone dabbling in stolen property and keeping late hours like the man I'd followed the night before would be a late riser.

He let me down.

When I got within a block of the house with the sign in the front yard advertising ROOMS, I saw a car that looked like the one I'd followed with Bartoz. It was pulling away from the curb. As it passed, I saw the license plate was the same.

Now I faced a dilemma. With the man who'd met Nick Perry gone, I could check names on the entryway mailboxes without running into him and risking the chance he'd remember me if he noticed me watching him later. Alternatively, I could follow him and see why he was out and about so early.

Following won.

He parked a block or so away from the soup kitchen where I'd met Punchy McKenzie. Drunks and derelicts and petty crime abounded here. A woman alone was bound to attract attention unless she was hunting customers or picking through garbage cans. It was early for the first and I wasn't dressed right for either. Nevertheless, I wanted to see what the man who walked with his elbows out was up to.

The DeSoto crawled along as slowly as it could without stalling. I passed him. If I parked to watch where he went, I'd stick out. If I looped around the block, I could lose him. At the intersection I swung onto the side street, stuck my arm out the window with frantic hand waggling, and brought the car to a stop. Hopping out, I raised the hood and peered anxiously at the engine. Sometimes acting like a fish out of water is the best way to blend in.

A car pulled around me, honking to warn me not to step out into the traffic. It was sparse where I'd turned. From my vantage point I could see a block and a half down the street I'd been on. Elbows-Out was still walking.

"Need some help there, honey?"

While I'd watched Elbows-Out, a bulb-nosed guy with more flab than muscles under his stained tweed jacket had crept within arm's grab on the curb side. Hard to say whether he intended to hit me up for money or snatch my purse.

"Yeah, take a peek under there and tell me what made my car conk out." I tossed him a quarter.

He fumbled and almost dropped it but didn't. His blink suggested he was startled to encounter composure rather than hand-wringing.

"Sure thing, honey. What's your name?"

"Arabella."

"Classy. It fits you."

The smile he bestowed on me looked more like a leer. I quickly was pegging him as a third-rate hustler instead of a threat. Coming a step closer, he eyed the DeSoto's engine with pretended earnestness. The Smith & Wesson felt cozy under my jacket. Across the way, Elbows-Out halted in front of a doorway.

"Looks to me like you have a leak in there, honey. I know a good mechanic."

Was Elbows-Out...? Yes. He was unlocking the door.

"There's a little place there we could go and have a beer while I called him," my knight in slimy armor suggested.

"You know, I bet I just flooded it." Stepping past him, I slammed the hood, causing him to jump away. "Don't know why I didn't think of that."

The DeSoto purred at my touch. I rounded the block in record time. As I passed the place Elbows-Out had just unlocked, someone inside turned a card in the single window from CLOSED to OPEN. The lettering on the window said USED BOOKS.

Dirty books, I wondered as I continued? That would be about right for this neighborhood. The thought of what might have rubbed off on pages of second-hand pornography was more than I could stomach. Regardless of what kind of volumes adorned its shelves, it would make a swell place for stashing stolen goods.

* * *

I was curious what went on at the bookstore, but I was equally curious about the man I'd followed there. With his whereabouts accounted for at least temporarily, I could have a quick look around the place where he lived.

On the way I pulled to the curb and replaced my suit jacket with a gray cardigan I kept in the trunk. I traded my peacock blue hat for a dismal gray cloche. When I got to my destination I parked half a block away and walked to the place with the sign in the front yard that said ROOMS.

Over one arm I had my muslin shopping bag. It would lend credence to my story of collecting old clothes for the needy if anyone happened along and questioned my presence while I checked the names Bartoz had been unable to read in the dark. No one did.

The rooming house was clean but utilitarian. Ten wooden pockets for mail, each with a bracket beneath, decorated one wall of its small entry. Numbers painted in black matched each box to a room. Most of the brackets beneath held slips of paper with hand lettered names. Two didn't. One was on the third floor.

When I'd climbed the stairs, it was no surprise to find the unidentified room was the one at the back. The one where a light had gone on after Bartoz and I followed Perry's pal there last night.

I knocked on the door, then the one beside it, but no one answered. I tried the door across the way and heard a voice call in response. After a moment a brunette in a satin wrapper opened the door a foot.

"Yeah?"

"Oh, hello. I'm supposed to pick up some clothes from Mr. Pennington for the parish rummage sale, but he doesn't seem to be at home." I gestured toward the door across the way.

"Pennington?" the brunette said irritably. "The guy over there's named Rice, and he wouldn't lift a finger to help anybody." She slammed the door.

Rice. At least I had a last name. Maybe.

I was in such a good mood I decided to head for the morgue.

FORTY

On the face of it, nothing connected the man who'd disappeared from The Canterbury to the one who'd died in a fleabag. Nothing except the fact the stiff in the fleabag had turned up a day or two after the one from the fancy hotel went missing. There was also what Smith had mentioned about the man's hands being callused, though that might mean nothing. Some well-to-do men went rowing and did other things that might give them calluses.

The coroner was a crusty old guy who cleared his throat and spit a lot. The crowd he hung out with probably didn't object. I'd been to see him a couple of times, but he acted as if he didn't know me from Eve. Maybe the disinfectants and such he inhaled every day had affected his memory.

"A-yeh. Here it is," he said, unearthing a file. His finger zig-zagged down a page as he read. "Still no name. You and the cops are the only ones to take any interest in him. Male. White. Late forties. Been bumming for some time, judging by scars and muscles and such. Looks like he got enough money somewhere to buy himself a couple of quarts of cheap whiskey and used it to wash down a handful of pills. That was that."

"And it was deliberate?"

"The pills say it was. Now and again I've gotten one who might not've realize how much booze they were pouring down their gullet — probably weren't intending anything but a good drunk. But mix in pills, especially that many...."

"Yeah."

I'd read about socialites or celebrities dying that way. Unless a note was left suggesting otherwise, those were usually passed off, in public at least, as "accidental". The thing that stuck in my mind about those was that most had been women.

"What about his liver and that? Had he been a boozer?"

The coroner examined his notes.

"No. I remember now thinking the liquor was probably more toxic because of it."

The will-o-the-wisp possibilities that had lured me here kicked into high gear.

"What else was unusual about him?"

"Unusual?"

"Don't lots of stiffs, especially John and Jenny Does, have something odd about them? Something that makes you wonder what their story is?"

Maybe the old duffer had no more curiosity than a stone. I was hoping to scratch his professional pride enough to squeeze out anything else he knew. He squinted in thought and drew up his top lip, exposing his teeth so he resembled a groundhog checking conditions before coming out of its hole.

"Well, he'd had a haircut recently, a good one, and his nails were trimmed. Kinda sad, with the rest of him so scruffy. A-yeh. There was his underwear, too."

"What about it?"

"Looked almost brand new. First quality. His socks too. You don't see many bodies where the outside clothes are all ragged but the ones underneath are that fine."

Unless you've been masquerading as a rich guy, and for some reason had to give your outer togs back.

* * *

When I got back to The Canterbury, the desk clerk called me over and handed me a message written in tidy script:

Movies at 7:30.

It didn't need a name, or the neatly added phone number.

Maybe by some miracle there'd be something useful in the footage Ione had shot. I was ready for a miracle. Meanwhile, I set off to find Frances. When I did, I handed her a set of photographs.

"Sorry, I don't recognize anyone. Should I?"

After considerable sweet talking, the coroner had agreed to let me borrow one of John Doe from the flophouse and one of another stiff, mainly because some sort of muck up had resulted in extra prints which he could afford to lose if I didn't return them. I'd added one from my files which showed a man sleeping so soundly he could have been dead.

"I was hoping one of them might be the man who disappeared," I said.

"Oh." Her worried look eased. "I never saw him. He came and went while I was still under orders to be an invalid, not leave the apartment and that...." Her voice trailed off. "I've said I was fuzzy before, haven't I? I suppose I ought to explain."

She glanced at me, hoping I'd say she didn't need to. I didn't. We were near what proved to be a storeroom heaped with small pedestal tables. She motioned me in and left the door open an inch so she could see out.

"We wanted a family so badly, Joshua and I. A baby. But every time it started to look as though we might, I had a miscarriage. The last time... the last time, I hemorrhaged. They... when I woke up, I'd... they'd given me..."

"A hysterectomy."

She nodded. "They'd told Joshua I might die if I didn't. If I became pregnant again. They kept me doped up. Not so much for pain from the surgery, but because I cried all the time. They told me to rest, get my strength back, leaving me with nothing to do except think. Finally Joshua moved me to a – a sanitarium. That was better but—. Anyway. Finally I got back here.

"Joshua's wonderful, but he smothered me, always telling me to rest, not letting me do things. And the pills I was supposed to take for my nerves made me woozy. When Polly died, I realized Joshua needed me, so I took hold and dumped out the pills, and at least I'm thinking better. But when that man was here, the one who vanished…" She spread her hand helplessly.

"I'm sorry," I said. "But I haven't wondered about that half as much as I have about what it is you've been holding back about who might have it in for you and your husband."

She opened her mouth to deny it, then sighed instead.

"I expect you're better at reading people than I am at a poker face. When I was determined to be a dancer, I ran off with a man in a band. He said he could introduce me to people. He didn't, and once he'd gotten what he wanted, he dumped me. After Joshua and I were married, the vile snake called one day claiming he had naked pictures of me, and would give them to Joshua unless I sent money to a post office box. Like an idiot I did. I've never heard from him since, and a few years later I told Joshua."

"But you think he might have crawled out of the woodwork."

I tried to reassure her even as I groaned inwardly at the prospect of another lead to follow. Then I tracked down Tucker in the dining room. We went to his office. I spread the pictures on his desk. He stood staring at them a long moment.

"That's him. The guy who vanished." His finger tapped the picture of the man from the flophouse. He looked at me with something approaching awe. "How'd you find him? Is he… uh, these all look like they're dead."

"The one with his head on the desk's asleep on the job. But the man who stayed here — let's call him JD — yeah, he's dead. Now that you've confirmed it's him, I'll start trying to find out how he ended up where he did. Now I have to ask you something. Frances told me about a man who tried to blackmail her over some pictures."

"Yeah?" The set of his jaw said he didn't appreciate talking about it.

"What are chances he's got something to do with the trouble you're having?"

His round face split in a grin.

"Zero plus zero. Jealous husband shot him dead while he was on stage in front of a room full of people."

"When?"

He pulled at his chin.

"Four or five months ago. When Frances was in the hospital. It was in a couple of the theater rags I get in the mail."

Maybe he hadn't told her. Maybe she'd been too doped up to remember. Either way was one less problem for me.

I slid the photographs I'd shown Tucker back into my purse. If only I had a similar set of pictures with Nick Perry in it to show to Skip and the clerk from Lagarde's. I was willing to bet Skip, at least, would be able to identify him, which would be exactly the kind of evidence that might light a fire under Freeze.

The thought halted me. I had a camera. A nice little Kodak. All I had to do was run get it. And hope unlikely lovebirds Lena and Nick showed up for lunch.

* * *

"What exactly is it you want me to do?" Frances asked as we walked toward the dining room where lunch was now in full swing.

"Unfold the measure about four feet and hold it up where I tell you to, like I'm taking pictures to analyze later. Don't worry whether you're doing it right. We're just setting it up so no one in there thinks anything of it if I ask them to hold something later."

"Oh. All right. It's just that I look awfully frumpy to be in a picture."

"You can burn them yourself, if you want. I'm not going to use them."

Perry and his girlfriend hadn't been anywhere in evidence when I rushed to my office to get the camera. They now shared a table for two by the wall. Menus beside them suggested they hadn't yet ordered. Each had a martini. Liquor hadn't sparked amorous displays, or even conviviality.

"Now, if you'll just stand right there at the end, it will give me a base measure," I ordered Frances. I opened the front of the Kodak and pulled the pleated leather bellows out on its track. "Unfold the ruler four feet up and down and hold it snug to the wall — one hand only. Good."

I pressed the shutter release. The flashbulb flared. A film roll for my camera gave me eight shots, so I took two more with Frances and one at another table. Then I approached Lena and Nick.

"Would you mind awfully each taking an end of this while I take two fast pictures?" I asked Lena. "I'm measuring service angles."

"Oh, I suppose not." She sounded out of sorts as she took the folded ruler from my hand. I'd left two sections open.

"For God's sake, Lena. Why should we?" Perry grabbed the ruler and thrust it back at me so forcefully the tip nearly hit his companion's glasses. "If you need an assistant, hire one. We're here to have lunch. Quit bothering us."

"Don't be such an ass, Nick. We haven't even ordered yet. Maybe you're in a hurry to get back to that narrow-minded old woman. I'm not." She snatched back the ruler.

"Goodness. I've never seen anyone make such a fuss over having their picture taken." I spoke to Perry as if he were a child or less than bright. "I can't ask any of the Hollywood people. The risk of recognition might skew the research. I need someone whose appearance won't attract a second look."

Dislike flooded Perry's eyes. Lena's mouth pursed with enjoyment.

"Oh, dear. That's a problem. You see, Nick fancies himself quite handsome—"

"Shut up." He caught the other end of the folding ruler. "Take your picture."

"Oh, thank you! If you'll both lean back with one arm on your chair, and hold your end of the measure in line with your ear...."

Snap and snap. I took one picture in her direction and one in his, making sure to include both of them in each shot.

FORTY-ONE

Usually it took three or four days between dropping off film and getting back pictures. Fortunately, I had an arrangement with Ernie.

"Ah, the lovely Miss Sullivan." He slid photos and negatives from one of the stacks before him into an envelope, which then went into a basket of orders awaiting pickup. "And with that look that tells me you're here to put extra change in my pocket."

In the front of his place, Ernie had a perfectly respectable business for printing folks' snapshots. In a back room he took pictures of women whose only attire was a gauzy scarf or a couple of ostrich plumes. Our arrangement was that so long as I didn't rat on his illicit enterprise, he'd turn out pictures for me in a day when I needed it. The second part of the arrangement was paying twice his usual fee.

"Don't you think you should wear a mask when you hold people up?" I gave him my film.

"Late as it is, I can't get these to you today. Midmorning tomorrow?"

"Yeah, okay. Nine-thirty? Make me two sets."

* * *

The flophouse, when I found the address Connelly had given me, was still telling itself it was a hotel. The single word clung to the front in fading paint without a name to accompany it. The street in front made Polly Bunten's neighborhood seem stylish in comparison. The has-been hotel was as far removed from The Canterbury as the war in Europe was from Dayton.

For several minutes I stared with distaste at the place I was about to enter. No doorman here. No front steps either. Just a threshold of rotting wood. Strips of tape patched a crack in the wavy front window.

Inside, the smell of disinfectant lost its battle against the odor of seldom washed bodies and other things I didn't want to identify. Behind the reception desk on my left, a sign informed prospective guests the nightly rate included sheets. An extra two cents got you soap and a towel.

"You selling something?" The man behind the desk eyed me sourly. His open shirt collar showed a beefy neck and florid complexion.

"Buying." I put a dollar down. "What can you tell me about this man? Died in one of your rooms about a month ago."

He barely glanced at the morgue picture.

"Don't remember him."

"A lot of your guests die, do they?"

"Now and then. 'Case you haven't guessed, we don't get the cream of society."

A woman clutching an armful of wadded-up sheets made her way down the stairs with a gait suggesting one leg was shorter. Her stained apron was the antithesis of the crisp, starched numbers worn by even the scrub maids at The Canterbury.

"Look, some people want me to find out whatever I can about him. They think he might have had family."

"I told the cops everything I remembered. Ask them."

"Trouble is..."

I leaned across the reception desk as though to confide. He leaned in too. I brought the side of my fist up under his chin so hard he bit his tongue.

"...I'm here and I don't have much patience."

The beefy clerk howled and pawed his mouth, getting blood on his fingers. He settled on holding his jaws. The maid with the dirty linens had paused. Now she hurried unevenly past, pretending not to notice a thing.

"I don't like being here any more than you like having me. Answer my questions and show me the room where he stayed and I'll leave you alone," I said through my teeth.

The clerk's eyes were welling with tears.

"You almost cut my tongue in two, you know that?"

"Then you'd better start talking before I finish the job."

"There's nothing to tell about him! Nothing different from all the others. Didn't have to go through all his pockets to see whether he could afford the room like lots do."

The last few words gurgled. Grabbing wildly for a battered wastebasket, he spit out bloody saliva. It reminded him of his grudge against me. He scowled.

"That's it. All I remember. That and he got high and mighty about my towels."

"High and mighty how?"

"Said they didn't deserve to be used for anything except rags. His sullen tone, along with his words, confirmed my growing feeling he owned the dump.

As I looked at the dull gray stack on a shelf behind him, I agreed with the dead man. What guests here got as towels were paper thin, their hems worn to fringe. Someone who'd just had the use of white ones that were fluffy and thick might resent the contrast.

The clerk took out a handkerchief considerably cleaner than the surroundings and dabbed at his tongue as he led the way up the stairs — no elevators here. The place had two floors of rooms slightly larger than closets. The one where John Doe had stayed was halfway along on the top floor. Like all the others, its only furnishings were an iron bedstead with a stained mattress, a wooden chair and a clothes hook. A bathroom at the end of each hallway served the rooms on that floor.

The unrelenting bareness offered only one place for hiding something. As much as I hated to, I lifted the mattress and looked underneath. All I saw was stains and a dead roach. Any visible scrap left behind by JD would have been thrown out, or snatched up by subsequent occupants of the room.

Maybe JD had simply decided to end his life. Maybe we'd never know why he'd spent a few days at The Canterbury and left an empty envelope in the safe. I started back down with the desk clerk, feeling glum.

"Any women stay here?" Women noticed things. They talked more. They might be moved by my story the dead man had kin, which was probably true.

"Now and then. If they're paired up with some man. Don't see one alone more'n once a year, maybe."

The maid with the short leg was picking her way to the front door as she buttoned her coat. Around her the floor showed streaks of wet from a recent mopping.

"No hookers?"

"Not staying here, if that's what you're asking. Can't control who visits. Myrt." He raised his voice to the maid. "Did you clean that mess in the second floor toilet up good?"

She turned to face him.

"As good as I could with it overflowing every time you turn around."

"Bud's fixed it twice."

"Maybe you need to get a real plumber in."

Before he could answer, she wobbled out. I gave the clerk one of my cards.

"If you remember anything useful, there's another buck in it."

"Yeah, sure."

I saw him drop the card in his wastebasket as I left. My best hope now was the pictures I'd get from Ernie tomorrow.

A lungful of clean outside air improved my mood. I took another for good measure.

"Miss?"

Looking around, I located the source of the soft call. It was the maid with the short leg. She stood several doorways down, pressed against a vacant shopfront. She peeked to reassure herself she couldn't be seen from the flophouse. Her lower lip turned in to scrape her teeth as I walked toward her.

"Are you that lady policeman girls say is nice?"

"I'm not a cop. I'm a private detective. You know what that is?"

She nodded uncertainly.

"It means if you know something about that man I was asking about, I won't tell the police."

"Not me. Another girl might. I don't want to get her in trouble."

"It won't. What is it she knows?"

The maid shook her head

"I'm not sure." She peered nervously over her shoulder.

"Let's go around the corner."

She relaxed as we did.

"She saw somebody go to his room, I think. Day or two later, when she heard the man was dead and that the police had been there, she told Wally."

"The guy I met?"

"Yes. He told her to keep mum about it, that neither one of them needed trouble with the cops."

I thought a minute. The police would have talked to everyone who worked at the flophouse, meaning this other girl didn't.

"The girl who saw something, is she a hooker?"

"Yes." The maid looked awkwardly down.

"Some of the men who come there aren't so hard up. They just want a place so they don't have to... you know, in an alley. There's a few of the girls are okay. Not hard. Sylvia, a couple of times when I've had to work extra and come out late, she's seen me and walked a ways with me. Even gave me trolley fare once when she saw I was wore out."

"Well, I think you ought to have trolley fare for a week for sticking around to talk to me," I said handing her some change.

She hesitated. "I wasn't hinting."

"That's why I'm giving. This Sylvia, where can I find her?"

"Two, three doors the other direction when you leave the hotel. Not till eight-thirty or nine though."

FORTY-TWO

Rachel entered The Canterbury under full sail. The bouquet of roses filling her arms all but hid her. As she handed it to Smith, who'd stepped forward in anticipation he'd be needed, I saw her attire was subdued: Expensive black suit adorned by a gold lapel pin; a small hat, though she normally eschewed hats. Even the minks still chasing each other around her shoulders seemed to do so sedately.

"There's no guarantee Count Szarenski will see us," she said in greeting. "I left calling cards yesterday for him and his wife. I've received no reply."

"Maybe you should have sent the roses then."

Her lips gave the hint of a smile.

"I sent chocolates."

"Or perhaps they'd never received a card with 'construction' on it before and didn't know the proper form of address."

She slanted me a look, then slowly dipped into her pocket and flourished a card between two ruby fingertips.

It wasn't her business card. The creamy stock was thicker. The engraving on it was finer. Black script announced simply:

Miss Rachel Minsky

"My mother still entertains hope I'll turn out well," she said.

We'd reached the elevator. Smith spotted a room service waiter and murmured something which sent him scurrying. The pint-sized old bellman had clout.

"This might go better if I were alone," said Rachel as the elevator operator closed the folding brass gate.

"I want to watch their reactions."

"I can report the reactions."

"Two can watch better."

She shrugged. Did I detect a faint tension about her? I wondered if she was more in awe of Count Szarenski than she'd let on. Not of his title, perhaps, but of his stature with Poles on both sides of the ocean.

"I'll do social pleasantries first," she said as we rode up. "That I'm paying my family's respects etcetera."

We'd talked on the phone about what she'd say. She'd tell them I was working for the hotel. She'd say there were concerns their jewelry might not have been safe. I wasn't sure what I expected to learn, but at least it might help me eliminate one suspect, even one who seemed less and less likely. I needed to make sure the theory I'd worked out about Perry wasn't blinding me to other possibilities.

The ride to the second floor was short. Rachel fluffed her dark hair just before we stepped out. Bartoz stood with arms crossed by the room where we were headed. He studied Rachel with interest. When we were a few steps away, he rapped on the door next to him. A word from the other side, and he opened it with a flourish. Count Szarenski stood before us without his cane.

Rachel trotted out a string of words and inclined her head to almost a half bow. The ramrod straight count nodded slightly. He didn't reach for her hand to kiss it as he had the Frenchwoman's. I heard something vaguely resembling my name, and the count looked at me. I rated a blink.

Speaking again, he gestured toward the blonde woman with him, whom I took to be his wife. Rachel jabbered and gave her the roses. The room service lad hustled up the back stairs in time to hold out a crystal vase. The door closed behind us. Bartoz was excluded.

The suite we entered, as Frances had hinted, made cramped living space for four people who spent little time downstairs. No personal items were in evidence, only a silk upholstered settee, small tables and a couple of chairs. Next to the room's single window, which looked out on the alley, a pair of straight chairs flanked a table for two with a skirt that matched the draperies.

I couldn't make heads or tails of the conversation around me. The dark haired woman and the girl who liked to glare took the flowers and vase to the table. Rachel seated herself across from the count and his wife while I took a chair out of their line of sight.

Talk ensued. All at once the blonde made a mewling sound and pressed a hand to her mouth. Count Szarenski's erect bearing melted. His thumb stroked her cheek. He spoke softly, as if in reassurance.

Rachel's words to me were as tight as her face.

"They had three stones changed out in Cuba on the way over. They needed the money."

The twosome at the window had turned curiously at the unfolding drama. A word from the count sent them into a bedroom. His wife leaned into his shoulder. He kissed her hair. He made a shooing gesture at Rachel. We left.

"They didn't know about the bracelet?" I said when we were in the hall again. There was no sign of Bartoz.

"No. They were counting on that and a third piece they brought to bankroll them if worse came to worse." She jabbed the elevator button with a lacquered fingertip.

"I don't get it," I said. "Why would a thief steal only from Europeans and interventionists like Lena Shields?"

"Maybe he has political leanings."

"Have you ever met a crook who cared about politics?"

"Only the ones who were politicians." She jabbed the button again.

"Have we earned a drink?"

"Yes. No. I need to be alone, I think. I'm more affected by that man and his family than I anticipated. If I could find the s.o.b. who did this, I would kill him."

* * *

I updated my clients and managed not to slug Joshua when he again refused to listen to reason and hire someone to watch the safe.

I drove to the Jenkins' apartment where we all watched what Ione dubbed her 'debut movie'. It seemed a lot shorter than when we'd walked around making it. Three times through it confirmed that a small portion of the lounge would be invisible to someone peeking from Tucker's office to check if the coast was clear. As far as I was concerned, that was all it showed. No suspicious characters skulking around or doing anything odd. And, alas, no passing glimpse of Nick Perry that could prompt a witness to leap up and say, "That's the man with the moles!"

At a quarter past nine, I made a slow circuit of the block with the flophouse. No ladies of the night were in evidence, or at least none in quest of clients. I went around again, zig-zagging onto an unpaved lane to finish the loop without backtracking. As I neared the spot where Sylvia was said to do business, I slowed. Two women in tight skirts and too much makeup, one of them leaning against the wall, were chatting. I pulled to the curb.

The one who wasn't leaning looked up. I let the DeSoto's engine idle. She sauntered over. When she reached the passenger side, I cranked down the window.

"Are you Sylvia?"

Startled I wasn't a man, she jerked back. I waved a two-dollar bill.

"This is yours if you send her to me."

"Get out. Sylvia's not that kind."

"I just want to talk—"

"Scram before I yell for Bartholomew!" Her voice had gone shrill. She stumbled backwards. "Nobody here does other women, you piece of filth. Scram!"

Stunned, I started to step from the car to show her just how scared I wasn't of Bartholomew. Then reason told me that near as I was to getting answers about the missing man, and possibly his link to troubles at The Canterbury, I shouldn't risk causing a ruckus which might draw attention.

Struggling to control my temper, I let out the clutch and drove on. At first my route was aimless. Soon thoughts as well as itinerary grew more orderly. I checked the second-hand bookshop. It was closed and dark. The dregs of society flowed through the streets around it.

The alley behind the bookshop was too narrow for cars. On the opposite side of the alley, its back facing that of the bookstore, an industrial laundry kept its sliding doors open to let out heat from the presses. The light and bustle there made chances of illegal activity through the rear of Rice's shop just about zero.

Next I checked Rice's rooming house. His Chevy was outside. The light in his room was on. I sat and watched for a while, but impatience to come up with a way to talk to the hooker named Sylvia made me fidget.

I needed to swallow my pride and ask a man to help me. Not Connelly. Running to him every time I needed something would make me feel weak. Pearlie would help, but having him ask about someone would more likely send the person he asked about into hiding. Pearlie wasn't bad looking, but something in his manner told you what he was. Or had been before Rachel hired him. Besides, I didn't have a way to reach him except through Rachel.

The light in Rice's room went out. I waited. He didn't emerge. It was too late for him to be heading out to the bar where he'd met Nick Perry, and hours early for him to catch any bundles dropped from The Canterbury.

That was when I thought of the perfect recruit for my new hunt for Sylvia.

FORTY-THREE

Bartoz was in his stocking feet when he opened his door. He seemed startled to see me.

"I'm sorry to disturb you so late," I said softly. Mrs. Avery across the hall might be sleeping by now. The Szarenskis might be as well.

"No, it's fine." He hesitated. "Will you come in?"

I did, and gestured to close the door. His bed was neatly made, so he hadn't been sleeping. It wasn't completely unlikely he slept on the floor to listen for hall noises.

"I need your help for an hour or so if you're willing. If you think it's safe to leave the count."

He hesitated. "Yes. He needs to feel he can protect his family. Inside the hotel is safe, as you said yesterday. Help how?"

"I need you to help me find a hooker."

Bartoz stared, sure he'd misunderstood.

"Hooker," he repeated. I could practically see him turning the word over, double-checking that he had the right meaning. "You mean a woman who, ah...."

"Yes. I need to talk to her."

"Ah."

"I asked another girl to send her over, but that girl got the wrong idea. Told me if I didn't leave she'd make a fuss."

"Let me put on my shoes," said Bartoz. "Will you wait?" He gestured toward the room's upholstered chair.

"Downstairs."

It would give him privacy to use the loo and tell the count he was going out, if he wanted to. Five minutes later we were walking toward my car.

"The count wishes that I tell you he didn't send you and the lady with roses away because he was angry," said Bartoz as we left the parking lot. "He did it because his wife was —"

"I understand. Neither one of us liked upsetting her."

I wasn't sure how much he knew about what we'd discussed.

"Much of it was her shame, you see. That people would know they have so little money."

"Is that why you go to the bank and the post office every day? The count's expecting some sort of payment?"

"Yes." Bartoz lowered his window halfway and lighted a cigarette. He flicked the match out the window. "I think he waits in vain."

I looked at him sharply.

"When Poland started to crumble, Count Szarenski sent some of his funds to Lyons. There was a trustworthy man, a banker, so circumspect it seemed unlikely the Nazis would notice him. He was to send a bank draft here, but...."

"You think he put the money in his own pocket?"

"No," said Bartoz flatly. "I think he's dead."

We were on Third now, headed to Ludlow, from which we'd make our way to the warren of streets that led to the flophouse. We didn't speak again until we were almost there. Then I told him what I wanted, and left it to him how to handle it.

When I began to pull over, he rolled the window down and hung his elbow out. Almost at once, a woman appeared from the alley, if the darkened footpath between the hotel and its neighbor deserved such a name. She was harder looking than the one who'd sent me packing. Her hips swayed as she came to the car.

"Are you Sylvia?" asked Bartoz, leaning out. "I'm told Sylvia's very kind with men who are unattractive." His voice projected unexpected charm.

"She's with a customer. I can be real kind too."

"A lovely invitation, but Sylvia was recommended to me. I'll wait. Perhaps you could let her know?"

The hooker noticed me now. Bartoz waved a hand in dismissal.

"My driver. She's unimportant."

A man came up the sidewalk, jingling the change in his pocket. The hooker lost interest in Bartoz. She nodded toward the flophouse.

"Sylvia went in there. She could be awhile." She set course for the jingling man.

"How will I recognize her?" called Bartoz.

"Yellow sweater," she answered over her shoulder.

There wasn't much traffic where we were. Few in this neighborhood could afford cars. I pulled the DeSoto to the curb and parked. Staring at the flophouse, I wondered whether Sylvia liked going inside better than servicing men in the alley, or if she simply went along with her customers' wishes.

"That place is a pigsty," I said.

Bartoz nodded. "I've been in similar places. When I was young." He probably wasn't much older than I was. He looked moodily out the window. "I suppose I'll have to resort to that again, though in nicer surroundings, if I want female companionship now. With this."

He flicked a finger toward his disfigurement. I managed to hold my tongue for a minute.

"Actually, Bartoz, if you'd trade the patch you wear now for a black one, I'll bet you'd have all kinds of women flirting with you."

He turned to me in disbelief.

"Flirting! But—"

"It will make you look mysterious. Dashing. Like men they've seen in the movies. Duels. Pirates—"

He gave a bark of amusement.

"Pirates."

We could be waiting a long time. I switched to easier subjects.

"Why does the Szarenski girl keep scowling at me?"

"Julitta?" He took out his cigarettes and rocked the pack between his fingers so long the silence became heavy. "She's a sweet girl, really. One who's been forced to see — and do — terrible things. She frowns to protect herself, I think. To keep people away. I think, too, she's jealous of you. Your car. Your independence. How you look. And..." He sighed. "She crushes on me."

"Crushes? Has a crush on you, you mean? Is smitten?"

"Yes. She— Is that sweater yellow?"

He threw the pack of cigarettes onto the seat.

Before I could look he was out of the car, leaving the door ajar and approaching a woman who'd just emerged from the flophouse. I'd given him greenbacks. Bartoz dangled them from his fingertips as he spoke to her. When they drew abreast of the car and he started to steer her toward it, Sylvia dug in her heels.

"Hey, are you crazy? I'm not getting in a car. The lane or the hotel. That's it. Period."

Bartoz caught her arm. I leaned across the seat and pushed the door wider, hoping she could see me.

"Sylvia. All you have to do for your money is tell me about the man who died in the hotel there — what you saw that night."

She was struggling and the sight of me didn't help much.

"I didn't see—"

"Yeah, you did."

Her brown hair was curled and fluffed and tangled, with a black bow holding it up on one side. Her yellow sweater was tight. The neckline wouldn't protect her from chest colds.

"I was at the hotel today. I'm a private detective. The guy who runs it doesn't know I know about you. I'm not here to make trouble. Talk to me for ten minutes and you get your usual fee now..." I nodded at Bartoz, who held it out invitingly. "...and the same again when we're finished.

"If that arrangement doesn't suit you, I'll have to talk to the cops. They'll make your life awfully unpleasant."

She swallowed.

"Sylvia?" A man stepped out of the alley. He was thickset and not much more than a shape, the street was so meagerly lighted. "What's going on there?"

"I'm negotiating," she snapped, whirling as much as possible with Bartoz holding her arm. "Keep your nose out." She turned back to me. "Not here. Somebody might put two and two together."

"What about if I buy you lunch tomorrow?"

"The Woman's Club?" Her laugh was harsh.

"Anyplace you want."

"How about Pixies? One o'clock."

She all but ran toward the alley.

* * *

Bartoz and I didn't talk much on our way back to the hotel. We hadn't taken half a dozen steps into the lobby when something in my peripheral vision jerked me from thoughts about whether Sylvia would keep our appointment.

Light from Tucker's office outlined the door, which was open a crack. It was after midnight, time for it to be locked and dark. I stopped at the foot of the stairs.

"I need to talk to Mr. Tucker a minute. Thanks for helping tonight, Bartoz."

Snapping as erect as the count, he gave me the same half-bow the count had bestowed on Rachel. When he was partway up the stairs, I moved toward the door with the safe. With the light on I didn't expect to find a robbery in progress. What worried me was the possibility something else had gone missing.

Instead, as I reached the door, I heard laughter. Knocking softly, I nudged the door open, then stopped in surprise. Frances, Eulahbelle Avery, Veronica Page and one of the male dancers sat at a table arrayed with cards and poker chips.

"Maggie!" Frances greeted me with a Cheshire Cat smile. "Come in. Shall I deal you in?"

"You'll lose your shirt and be here til breakfast trying to get it back," Veronica cautioned. "I've played with her before."

"I was fool enough to once in London," chimed in Eulahbelle. "Four o'clock, five in the morning before it ended."

Glasses and liquor bottles were contributing to the merriment. Frances' eyes met mine.

"I don't play often, but when I get started, I'm one hell of a poker player."

FORTY-FOUR

Frances' ploy of staging a poker game to make sure no one got into the safe was dazzling. I was out and about too early the next day to congratulate her. I took the borrowed pictures back to the coroner, along with muffins from The Canterbury to sweeten him up for future favors. I picked up the prints of the photographs I'd taken at the hotel. The morning could still pass as young when I arrived at Skip's theatrical shop.

"That's him. He's the one."

Skip tapped one of the photographs I'd spread before him on his display case. It was easier finding pictures of live people than of dead ones, so I'd given him half a dozen.

"You're sure?" I asked.

"Absolutely. Before we started this place, I spent enough years helping actors put on makeup to know how a face looks with and without additions. Add a couple of moles and a mustache, and that's the man who came in."

He'd picked out the picture of Nick Perry.

"Then what I want you to do is draw those in on one of these."

Rummaging until he found a pencil that suited him better than the one on his counter top, Skip added the details of Perry's disguise so subtly it took several looks to recognize they weren't part of the original. I now had two copies of the identical photo, showing the same man. In one he appeared as described by Skip and the clerk from Lagarde Jewelers; in the other as he looked at The Canterbury.

"You're some artist," I said in admiration.

Ship hooked thumbs under his red suspenders and tried not to show he was pleased. I put the pictures away.

"May I use your phone?"

* * *

Freeze was in some kind of meeting. It should be over in forty minutes or so, I was informed. Meantime, there was another phone call I wanted to make, one better made where I had more privacy. I thanked Skip and left, with the glorious feeling I was finally making progress.

The dead plant in my office had long ago become part and parcel of my decor. The sagging window shade was entirely different. When I opened the door, the sight of it still hanging listlessly irked me as much as it had the first time the shade refused to roll up. I turned my back on it and its perkier neighbor, divided the mail I'd brought in between desk and wastebasket, and located Sarah O'Neill's phone number.

"This is Maggie Sullivan," I said when she answered. "I came by asking questions about your cousin yesterday. How's your little boy?"

"He's... better, thanks."

"I thought it would be less disruptive if I called instead of coming over again." It was a nudge to encourage her to cooperate now. I didn't give her long enough to speak. "There's something I forgot to ask when I was there."

"Yes?"

Talking to me didn't appear to be the highlight of her day.

"The boy you remember Nick palled around with — the son of a chauffeur or gardener — what was his name?"

The silence lasted so long I thought she was going to hang up, but she didn't.

"I can't remember. Honestly. I saw it in the paper six or seven years ago — he'd been arrested for something. I recognized it then, but now...."

"Why was he arrested?"

"Not for murder or anything dreadful like that. It just caught my eye because of the name. It had something to do with a house, I think."

"Uh..."

"Couch? No. Draper? No."

I got what she meant now.

"Butler?" I suggested. "Cook?"

"No... but I do think it might have to do with a kitchen."

"Baker? Lamb?" A thought stabbed into me. "Rice?"

"Yes! That's it! Colin — no, Kevin — Rice!"

* * *

I called to see whether Freeze was out of his meeting. Boike answered and told me he was. Five minutes into my visit, Freeze held up a hand.

"You're telling me the dead bum in that flophouse is the same guy who disappeared from the fancy hotel?"

"Yep." I sat back in my chair.

"Based on nothing except the say-so of the butterball who owns the place and one of his waiters?"

"And one of the bellhops, who's a sharp old bird. He picked the same man out of the photos. And he'd told me when I first asked that the man who'd vanished had callused fingers." I clasped my hands around my knees and leaned forward. "I'll bet he told your men too. And I'll bet the coroner told you about the stiff from the flophouse having new underwear."

Freeze shook out the match he'd just used. He took a draw on his cigarette.

"Lots of do-good groups collect socks and underwear. Give it out at the missions. Anyway, the guy wasn't a homicide."

"Philippe Lagarde was, and a clerk who came in early heard him arguing with someone — even got a look at whoever it was. Remember how she described him?"

"How did you—?" Freeze shot a suspicious look at Boike, who was jotting down notes at the desk to his right, then at another lackey who leaned on the edge of it. He started to reach for a file, then recited from memory. "Medium build, pair of moles by one eyebrow."

"And a medium mustache."

Freeze flipped the file open.

"Clerk never mentioned a mustache."

"Somebody else who met him did." Reaching into my purse, I took out the envelope with the photographs I'd taken the day before. "And if you show the clerk, she'll tell you it's him."

I flipped the one Skip had doctored onto his desk. Freeze bent over it with interest. Suddenly his expression sharpened.

"Is this your idea of a joke? Someone's drawn on this."

"Yes. And here's the original. This is how he looks when he doesn't stick on his disguise. He's a guest at The Canterbury."

Boike and the other guy crowded closer to look.

I laid it out for them: How Nick Perry had gone into Skip's hunting someone to copy jewelry; his local roots; his youthful safe cracking. Freeze squashed out the stub of his cigarette.

"Long way from enough to charge somebody with murder," he said sourly. "If that cuckoo you're working for had reported thefts from his safe, it might be different."

"They reported a dead girl stuffed in a trash can. She scrubbed floors in the middle of the night, Freeze. Down on her knees where she wouldn't be seen until she popped up when Perry was going in or out of the room with the safe. He didn't want a witness, so he killed her."

"You *theorize*."

Frustration drove me out of my chair. I rounded it and gripped the back to control my anger.

"What about the Lagarde case? A witness saw Perry arguing with him the day he was murdered. Doesn't that at least suggest a motive? A possible one, worth exploring? It gets you off the hook if I'm wrong."

Giving him the satisfaction of hearing me raise that possibility stuck in my craw, but time was running out at The Canterbury. Lily Clarke was leaving on Sunday. Unless I could stop it, her diamonds would be gone before then, and the Tuckers would be ruined.

The phone rang. Freeze answered, listened a minute, then thanked someone. He jotted something on a notepad next to the phone and tore off the top sheet.

"I'll think about it," he said. He reached for the suit jacket draped on the back of his chair.

"I'm not done."

"Miss Sullivan, we have things to do."

"Does the name Kevin Rice ring a bell?"

Freeze was bullheaded, but waving the red flag in this direction might get his attention. The name didn't register, so he looked at his two assistants. Boike nodded.

"Yeah. From when I worked robbery-burglary. He was a fence. Got sent away for a couple of years."

Freeze stood up, shrugging into his jacket.

"So?" He was looking at me.

"So he and Perry were pals as teenagers. So every couple nights since Perry's been at The Canterbury, he's dropped things out the hotel window to Rice. Nights they don't play that game, the two of them meet in a bar on Cass. Rice gives Perry something. Rice runs a used book store on Wayne, south of Fifth, a swell spot for dealing in stolen goods in case his stretch behind bars didn't turn him into a choirboy."

Freeze stared, the cigarette in his lips forgotten as the match in his fingers burned down.

"South of— what were you doing in a place like that?"

My patience snapped.

"Having tea. Contrary to what you think, Freeze, I don't spend my time with my feet on my desk eating bonbons while men toss information into my lap. I was following Rice."

The flame of the match reached his flesh. He swore and dropped it, batting it off the edge of his desk before it set any papers ablaze.

"There may be a thing or two there worth looking into if nothing else pans out," he relented. "Don't get your hopes up."

FORTY-FIVE

I don't know what prompted my next actions. Maybe it was letdown over Freeze's lukewarm response to my carefully connected dots. Or the contrasting memory of Connelly's belief in my abilities. Or simply my festering knowledge that by not doing something right, I was doing wrong. Whatever the reason, I drew several breaths, started my car, and set out to do what I'd been avoiding all week.

Actually, I'd been avoiding it since my father's death.

And so I drove, devoid of the mix of comfort and loss I usually felt, back toward my old neighborhood. Past the house I'd grown up in. Past the one where Wee Willie had lived, and still did with Maire and their rambunctious brood. I stopped in front of the narrow, two-story blue house I hated.

For several minutes I sat in front of it, drowned in emotion. Finally shame at my selfishness drove me up the walk. I turned the doorbell. I waited. The door opened.

There stood Maeve Murphy.

My father's paramour.

"Maggie!" The word was little more than a whisper. She leaned against the doorjamb. "Oh, Maggie, lamb. Not a day's gone by I haven't prayed you'd show up like this." Her eyes were damp.

She was still pretty. Trim. Her black hair showed the scattering of white to be expected in someone the age of my parents. The only thing she no longer had was the merriness I'd associated with her.

"I expect you've come for your dad's pipes," she said.

"Yes."

"Will you come in?"

I shook my head.

She smiled sadly, studying me with longing. "I won't be a minute."

When she was out of sight, I sagged against the nearest post of her small front porch. I'd adored Maeve once. When our paths crossed at church or parish functions, she would talk to me, ask what I liked best in school, how I got this scrape or that. Wee Willie's mom and Billy's wife Kate had chided me for biting my nails to the quick. My own mother was indifferent. Maeve had used a different strategy.

"You've such lovely hands, Maggie," she'd said one day after Mass. *"You should fix them up pretty and show them off. Here's emery boards for smoothing down your poor nails instead of chewing, and some pretty pink polish. Shall I put some on now?"*

And she had, our hands resting on a gravestone as she'd filed and fussed and showed me the best way for brushing on color. For the first time in my life, I'd felt pretty.

Then, several years after my mother died, I'd overheard gossip. Yes, my dad acknowledged when I confronted him, the couple of times each week he went out in the evening, he went to see Maeve. They were friends. He liked talking to her.

In my eyes, she'd become not so much a harlot as a thief. She'd stolen part of him from me. She'd taken part of the only person who'd ever loved me.

"I've cared for them the best I knew how."

Her voice startled me. I wondered how long she'd been standing there with the familiar old canvas valise, the sight of which made my throat swell.

"I rubbed saddle cream into the bag and the bellows, and opened the lid of the box he kept the reeds in," she went on. She cradled the valise against her as tenderly as Sarah O'Neill had cradled her fussing baby. "He used to do that. Open it up so the reeds could get some moisture from the air and not dry out."

She held out the bag.

"I hate giving this up, to tell you the truth. It's like letting go of the last little part of him."

"Thanks. For keeping it."

I turned to leave.

"Maggie — will you come back sometime? For tea or a whiskey? There are things I'd like to tell you."

"No."

I'd gone a couple of steps when her voice reached out to me a final time.

"He never loved any woman except your mother, Maggie. You need to know that. As long as she was alive, the two of us never — we were never together."

I nodded. I knew it wasn't enough, but it was all I could manage.

* * *

Maybe my stop at Maeve's would count as some sort of penance and Sylvia would keep our appointment. I clutched at the thought as I walked into Pixies. Given my failure to spur Freeze to action with the evidence I already had, the prostitute was starting to look like my last hope.

The restaurant was a plain but cheerful little place with ruffled chintz curtains framing windows that let in lots of light. Tables and chairs were knotty pine glistening with varnish. They didn't serve liquor but they had several daily specials, and soups and sandwiches as well as desserts. It was too far south on Main to attract the downtown crowd, but I'd been there a few times.

I arrived five minutes early. The bulk of the lunch crowd had already thinned out, and continued to leave, which was maybe why Sylvia had chosen this time. She came in right on the dot.

We almost didn't recognize each other. When we'd met, I'd been inside a car on a dark street, and she'd been decked out for business. Today her face was scrubbed clean of makeup. Her hair was brushed smooth and pulled back in a small knot at the nape of her neck. In her tan dress and sweater she fit right in here.

I smiled. She seesawed a thumb on the handles of her purse. After an endless second, she joined me, sitting shyly on the edge of her chair.

"I used to meet my sister here sometimes." She avoided my gaze. "Before her kids got older and.... I guess she didn't want to explain an aunt like me. Now and then I come here by myself."

"It's pretty," I said.

She nodded. A bruise that wasn't very big but looked as though it might be fresh decorated her left cheek.

"Bartholomew give you that?" I guessed, hoping that was the name the other hooker had used as a threat.

Sylvia's mouth curved with amusement. "Yeah. Got sore when I told him I wasn't about to go off in a car with some one-eyed heebie-jeebie I'd never seen before. It does Bart good to get a little backtalk now and then. He never smacks very hard."

"I'm sorry, all the same. Thanks for coming."

"It eases my mind, telling someone. I knew I should when I heard the police had been around asking questions. That miser who runs the hotel said if I did, I'd just get myself in trouble. I knew how the cops look down on girls like me, so it was easier to just go along...." She halted. "You're not police. You said last night."

"That's right." I gave her a card. She looked at it for a minute, then turned it face down as the waitress came. We ordered.

"So what did you notice about the man at the hotel?" I asked when we'd regained privacy. "What did you think you should tell the police?"

"It may not amount to a hill of beans."

"That's okay."

"It's just that he had a visitor that night. A visitor with a quart of booze."

The man who'd died at the flophouse had met his demise through a combination of pills and liquor. A fact which might have occurred to Sylvia as well. I fought to keep from shouting out too many questions, from pushing her, from leading her.

"What did he look like?"

"The man who died? I only caught a glimpse of him, when he was letting his visitor in—"

"Not the man who died. The visitor. What did he look like?"

"Oh. Well, first of all, *he* was a she. The visitor was a woman."

FORTY-SIX

Our coffee arrived as I sat speechless. Sylvia added cream from a pretty blue pitcher to hers.

"Why don't you tell it your way," I said. "I'll try not to butt in too much."

Sylvia stirred her coffee, organizing her thoughts.

"There's a customer who looks me up every couple of weeks. He always wants to go inside. For the privacy. The hotel's a dump, but the sheets are clean. Look it, anyway." She shrugged. "We'd finished, so I left his room to use the toilet down at the end of the hall and head back outside. A woman was coming up the stairs. Something about her caught my eye.

"See, I know most of the girls who work around here. Recognize them, I mean. I didn't recognize her. She had a quart of whiskey in her hand, and I saw another one peeking out of a bag she had over her shoulder. Well, that one might not have been whiskey, but it was some kind of liquor, and that's a lot of booze. It made me curious, so I sort of ambled along to where she went."

"And she went to the room of the man who died?"

Sylvia nodded. "Who is he? Why are you trying to find out about him?"

"Nobody seems to know who he was. A couple of strangers gave him a place to sleep for a few nights. He took off without saying why or where he was going. The police weren't interested, so they hired me to find out whatever I could. The people he stayed with are concerned he might have had family."

Plenty of men had hit the road or the rails these past ten years, when businesses closed and jobs dried up. Some, like Polly's boyfriend, had left seeking opportunities. Others couldn't face the shame of not feeding their families. It was common enough that she accepted my explanation.

"Did you see her go into the mystery man's room?"

"Yeah." She smiled at my 'mystery man'. "Dawdling along like I was, I was worried she'd notice me, but she didn't look around once."

Sylvia paused as one of the daily specials slid in front of her.

"Isn't that pretty? The way they serve it? With that little bit of green on the side." She looked down shyly. "Thanks for bringing me here."

"You earned it. And let me give you the money I owe you, too."

She had manners, and a wistfulness about her that made me wonder what had driven her to the way she earned her livelihood. She tucked the money into her purse and took a bite of her veal patty.

"So the woman knocked on the mystery man's door," she resumed, "and he opened it, but not a whole lot — like he was wondering who it was. She said something to him. I couldn't hear what. I could see his face, though, and he looked kinda pleased and surprised both. He let her in and the door closed. I used the toilet and that's all I saw."

I let her enjoy her meal awhile before I began with my questions.

"When you said you knew all the girls who worked around the hotel—"

"I meant hookers. Yeah."

She looked me squarely in the eye.

"And that's what you think she was?"

Whatever Sylvia needed to see in my face, she found it. She considered a minute.

"She was trying to look like one of us," she said at last, "but she didn't. Her face was painted up like the side of a barn, but her hair was all smooth and brushed. Her outfit was right, if you know what I mean, but it looked like it came from Rike's or Thal's or someplace nice."

My pulse quickened. Why would a woman try to disguise herself as a prostitute and visit a man at a cheap hotel? Why would she go to his room with two quarts of liquor, only to have him subsequently turn up dead from drinking too much?

Maybe she really was a prostitute, a better class one. After all, John Doe had stayed at The Canterbury before checking in at a flophouse. He'd had money. Maybe he'd gone there to punish himself....

I couldn't even pretend to swallow that alternative.

"What else did you notice about her? What did she look like?" The prospect of another lengthy and possibly unproductive road to follow lowered my spirits.

"On the tall side. Light hair, blonde I'd say, but it was hard to tell." Frowning slightly, Sylvia buttered the roll that had come with her special. "I guess what made me notice her, besides not seeing her around before, was her having those two bottles. The way she hung onto the bannister coming up, and how she kept her free hand on the wall like she needed to steady herself when she walked down the hall, it looked to me like she already was pickled."

Or wasn't wearing glasses she needed, or...

Ideas pinged around me, fast and sharp as shots at a firing range. From the start of this case I'd been surrounded by women skilled at changing their looks with makeup and clothes because they'd worked on stage, or hob-nobbed with people who had. Two could qualify as tall. And blonde. One needed glasses. The other was given to wobbly spells.

Deliberately or otherwise, one was a murderer.

It didn't make sense. Yet I knew it had to be true.

In my purse were photos I hadn't needed to leave with Freeze, the nonessentials I'd snapped yesterday at the hotel in order to get the one of Nick Perry. They showed Frances and Lena and one of the other female guests. It wasn't much of a selection, but it would do to convince me if I was wrong.

I didn't expect to be.

My sandwich was tasteless. I let Sylvia enjoy the rest of her meal in peace. When we'd finished, I took the photographs that might yet be worth the extra price I'd paid Ernie to rush them out of my purse.

"This is a long shot," I said sliding three to Sylvia. "But look at these and see if you think any of them could be the woman you saw."

The hooker's face quickened with interest. She spread them out and looked. She nodded to herself. She switched the snapshots, studied them some more, stacked them and handed them to me.

"Like I said, she'd gone to town with her makeup, but that one on top was her."

FORTY-SEVEN

I bounded up the stairs at Market House and into Freeze's office. He wasn't there. Neither was Boike.

"Where are they?" I asked two other detectives who looked up from their desks in a far corner. They'd been there that morning. They knew who I meant.

"Got called out."

"Where?"

"Don't know."

"Come on, you heard them say the street at least."

"You know we can't say." The one talking to me stood up. "Want to leave a message?"

A notepad on the desk beside me caught my eye. I'd seen Freeze jot something on it and rip off the top sheet that morning. It was his scratchpad.

"No, that's okay," I said quickly. "Maybe you can help me with something else, though. I think I might have lost an earring in here this morning. Would you have a look around over there and see if it bounced?"

They looked down automatically, nice, helpful fellows. I snatched the pad and held it behind my purse where it wouldn't be seen.

"No? Well, I kind of figured it was lost for good, but worth a try. Thanks anyway. When Freeze gets back, tell him I need to talk with him. It's urgent."

* * *

Stealing police property probably wasn't the smartest thing I'd ever done. I sat in my car and tried to make out impressions left by Freeze's pencil. I couldn't. Chafing at the loss of time, I turned the nose of my own pencil on its side and rubbed the lead lightly over the notepad. Enough of a street name emerged for me to make out what it was, and part of a number as well. Sometimes when your heart is pure and the stakes are high, a little bit of crime does pay.

The street in question was about as far north as you could go and still be within city limits. I tried not to think of a clock ticking down as I drove. Surely what I had now would persuade Freeze to act. Lily Clarke and her diamonds were due to depart day after tomorrow. That meant Perry had only two nights left to nab them.

I slowed for a funeral procession.

When I reached the street I was hunting, I found I'd been wrong on the address. It didn't matter. Farther up I saw two police cars. One was a cruiser. The other was the unmarked number used by Freeze.

It was a quiet neighborhood. The cops weren't advertising their presence much. I parked a block away so I couldn't be accused of interfering and walked toward the cars. When I was three doors away, Boike came out of a handsome stone apartment building. His footsteps picked up as he saw me.

"What're you doing here?"

"I need to see Freeze. That stiff who drank himself to death in the flophouse — a witness saw one of the guests from The Canterbury taking him two quarts of booze in that rathole the night he died."

Boike stared. Then his blocky head started to shake.

"He's not going to listen. There's a girl in there who bled to death, and it looks like some quack used a coat hanger on her. On top of that, the boss asked a couple of boys in burglary to nose around at that bookshop you mentioned. They didn't find anything."

"*Freeze sent them there?*" My rising voice shattered the afternoon silence. "Damnit, Boike! He acted like he wasn't interested. Now they'll be looking over their shoulders!"

I left him standing there and ran for my car.

Boike hadn't deserved my anger, but here I was with all the pieces falling into place, and Freeze had mucked it up. Instead of using the photos I'd brought him, instead of showing them and talking to the witnesses I'd mentioned — and I'd given him Skip's name too — instead of doing that and then hauling Nick Perry in while the cops took a good look at his room and his movements, Freeze had sent detectives from a different unit to Rice's shop to look for stolen merchandise. Out of the sky blue.

It was more than enough to put a pair of crooks on guard. Worse, it would probably make them wonder if someone was onto them. Nick Perry had taken plenty of risks already. He might take another one, changing his pattern somehow to get Lily's diamonds. It was equally likely he'd skip town. Maybe his girlfriend would too. If they did, three murders would go unpunished.

Getting back to the hotel would take less time than stopping somewhere and finding a phone, then waiting while the desk clerk located one of the Tuckers. I pushed the DeSoto as hard as I dared without risking a stop for speeding.

The Canterbury looked tranquil as ever as I ran past the doorman in his buttons and braid. The lobby was empty. Smith was nowhere in sight. The whole place drowsed in that afternoon interval before guests started drifting down for pre-dinner drinks.

"Where's Mr. Tucker?" I asked the assistant desk clerk.

The urgency of my manner rattled him.

"I-I don't know."

"Mrs. Tucker?"

"I don't—"

"Never mind. What about Mr. Perry and Miss Shields? Are they still around?"

His shoulders wilted with relief.

"I just saw Miss Shields going into Mr. Tucker's office. Oh... that must be where he is."

By the lift of his voice, he probably gave a bright smile. I was already halfway to the office and didn't see.

At this time of day, the stretch of hall by Tucker's office was little used. I would have taken out my .38 regardless. I kept it close to my shoulder. If necessary, I'd apologize. I slammed the door open.

Nick Perry stood just out of range of it, casually reading a sheet of paper.

Someone on the other side of me stuck a gun to my head.

FORTY-EIGHT

"If you want the Polish kid to keep breathing, put the gun on the desk and don't make a peep."

A circle of steel against your skull tends to extend split-second decisions. Lena Shields held the gun. She was talking about the Szarenski girl. I didn't see any sign of the girl, but there was every chance it was more than a bluff. A chance I couldn't take. I did as instructed.

"What the hell are you doing here? With a gun? Never mind. There's no time," Perry snapped.

He'd already closed the door. He stepped swiftly back to the safe, which I now saw hung ever so slightly ajar. Swinging it open, he pulled out a jewelry case. In broad daylight.

"Get her out of here."

He opened the case. Diamonds flashed.

"Where?"

"The car. Get in with her."

"But—"

"We don't have time for anything better, Lena. She can play patty-cake with the brat. Put her gun in your purse." He worked methodically, opening cases and dumping their contents onto a cloth.

"What have you done to the Tuckers?" I asked.

"They're—"

"Shut up! Get her out of here now. Who knows when those yahoos could start dressing for dinner and come down to get something out of the safe."

Lena had to let go of my arm in order to pick up my Smith & Wesson, but I couldn't risk making a move. The sound of a shot would bring at least a couple of hotel employees running. This swell little pair of robbers already had killed three people who got in their way. This close to success, they wouldn't blink at killing a few more.

Pulling me close with her free hand as though we were best chums, Lena shoved her gun in my ribs. The long stole attached to one shoulder of her wool dress hid the weapon splendidly. I wondered if she'd dressed for the occasion.

"In case you're wondering, if you try to get smart out there, I'll shoot anybody I need to," she said into my ear.

"I wasn't."

Even after I knew she'd delivered booze to the man at the flophouse, I'd supposed Lena was Perry's dupe. The past few minutes had made me suspect they were equal partners.

I let her lead me, unresisting, through the lobby. For all I knew, my clients might both be dead. I'd failed them. Failed to save them from ruin as every valuable in the hotel safe was stolen in front of me. If I could manage one good thing in all of this, it would be to save a girl whose parents already had lost so much.

Smith was carrying bags up for an arriving couple and didn't even see me leaving. As my Siamese twin and I stepped out, Bartoz was returning from somewhere with a bag from which I caught the fragrance of fresh bread. He nodded and spoke. I inclined my head.

"Lieutenant Bartoz."

Under the fancy stole, Lena's gun pressed a warning. If Bartoz had recognized anything in my words but polite greeting, his face didn't show it. We moved on.

By the time we reached a Nash Ambassador parked at the rear of the hotel lot, Perry was out of the hotel and quickening his pace. He carried a big box of chocolates under his arm. I doubted it held any chocolates.

"If she tries anything, shoot her," he said.

He slid under the wheel.

Lena took my purse and told me to keep my hands between my knees. As we drove, she opened my purse and went through the contents.

"Keep your eyes on her," Perry snapped.

"Do you think I'm stupid? I'm watching her. She's got a badge in here. And a paper that says she's some kind of detective."

In case anyone snooped through my room again, I'd been keeping them in the trunk of my car. I'd taken them out in case I needed to show them to Sylvia.

"You're to blame for cops showing up at Kevin's this afternoon!" Perry hissed. The Ambassador swerved.

"The bookshop, you mean? Yep. And they've got proof you killed Lagarde."

"No, they don't, because Kevin did." He laughed nastily.

If I could distract Lena, I might be able to open the door and roll out before she shot me. There were several places they might have stashed the Szarenski girl, though, and who knew what shape she was in. Right now my captors held all the cards. If I wanted to help the girl, the first step was to stay alive myself.

* * *

It didn't take long to figure out we were headed to Great Aunt Clara Duke's place. I suddenly wondered if the pair of thieves I was riding with had done away with the old woman when they'd hit town. But no, I remembered Lena's sulks over being forced to endure her company.

Dusk was settling by the time we drove between the gateposts of the haughty old mansion with its deep front lawn and iron fence. Lights shone at a couple of windows. Perry drove the Ambassador around to the back. Another car was parked there too, a smaller and far less memorable Buick half a dozen years old.

"Wait here," he said tersely.

He got out. Producing a gun from under his jacket, he entered the house through the back door. A moment later, he reappeared with a man I recognized as Kevin Rice. Up close Rice had a thin face with a matching mouth.

"Who's she?" he asked as Perry opened the door on my side and yanked me out.

"The meddlesome bitch who sicced the cops on your place. She's been spying on us. She's some kind of detective."

"Spying!"

"Don't worry. She won't cause any more trouble."

He shoved me into Lena's tender care.

"No more than you're already in," I said. "Killing Lagarde and the maid at The Canterbury—"

"She was where she shouldn't have been."

"And the man Lena killed at that flophouse?"

"So what? He had a couple of glorious days before he died." Lena laughed.

"Shut up or I'll add the kid to the list!" Perry ordered, pointing the gun at me.

"You will anyway."

"Maybe, maybe not." Contempt curled his lips. "You want to gamble?" He opened the trunk of the Ambassador and spoke to Rice. "You take the kid."

Good thing I hadn't jumped out of the moving car to hunt the Szarenski girl. Rice hauled her out of the trunk, very much alive. She kicked like a mule. Her hands were tied behind her and she was gagged. Lena shoved me forward. I couldn't see much as I stole looks over my shoulder, but I heard a slap as the girl kept resisting. Someone will pay for that, I vowed.

The girl proved such a hellion Rice wound up carrying her. When he caught up with the rest of us in the kitchen, he set her on her feet.

"What are we going to do with them?" He was faintly winded.

"Depends. You find anything?"

"Yeah, five minutes before you pulled in. There's another safe down here in that breakfast room, behind the ugly painting."

"My, my," jeered Lena. "It seems Great-Auntie didn't trust you as much as you thought."

Perry ignored her bait, but a muscle on his jaw twitched.

"Lock those two up with the old witch while I see if that's where she put the rest of her jewelry. Then check all the other rooms on the second floor. There might be cash or God knows what else squirreled away. If I can't get into this other safe in fifteen minutes, we'll have to clear out with what we have. Someone at the hotel's bound to notice the kid or the jewelry missing by then."

"While you're busy down here, maybe we'd better look after that for you." Lena indicated the candy box filled with hotel valuables.

Perry shot her an angry look.

"Fine." He gave it to Rice.

Lena and the bookstore owner marched the two of us up a flight of gleaming stairs. My eyes took in details that might help us escape.

"What did you do with the housekeeper?" I asked. "Kill her too?"

"It's her day off."

"And the Tuckers?"

"Tied up in the attic above their apartment. Go do some of your stupid measuring."

She shoved me into a room to the right of the second floor landing so hard I fell. The Szarenski girl got the same treatment. Before I could get to my feet, the door slammed and a key turned. I tested the door and got a nasty laugh for my efforts.

We were locked in, with fifteen minutes or less for me to save both our lives. The first thing I did was remove the Szarenski girl's gag.

The first thing she did was spit on me.

FORTY-NINE

"Okay. I get the message. You don't like me." I put my palms out in surrender, and to ward off more spit.

But the girl's gaze had moved beyond me. I turned and looked.

We were in the sort of upstairs sitting room where ladies in bygone days had entertained close friends. The white-haired woman slumped head first on the silver tea service she'd been presiding over wasn't likely to do any more entertaining. I went to her side and felt for a pulse, but her skin was already cold.

The girl looked on without emotion. I tried to think.

"Look, Julie, Julia — I know I'm not getting your name right, but I can't quite remember — I know you can't understand what I'm saying. I know you're afraid. But we're going to get out of—"

"Not afraid. *Not afraid!*" She jerked her chin at the body. "Dead, yes? I see much dead. Soldiers come to house. They shoot. We too. I shoot. Bang, bang. Make dead—"

"Yes, good," I cut in, alarmed by her escalating intensity, and relieved we could communicate, more or less. "Bartoz told me you were very brave," I added.

The compliment, or the name of the man she had a girlish crush on, derailed her as I'd hoped it might.

"Bartoz talks of me?"

"Yes."

She swung from agitation to pouting.

"Bartoz thinks I am child!"

Precious minutes were ticking away.

"When you're a year or two older, he'll see you're not. But for that to happen, we've got to get out of here. Understand?"

"Get out, yes."

"Let me untie your hands."

Whoever had trussed her up (Lena probably) had used a silk scarf. Fragile as it was, the fabric was strong. It also allowed a knot both smaller and tighter than possible in a rope.

"Why did they take you?" I asked as I worked at it.

"Take?"

"Put you in their car."

The girl shrugged.

"I sit. They park car, see me."

She'd been sitting on a car in the parking lot, as I'd seen her do.

"They argue. Handsome man laughs, says I will be in... in..."

"Insurance?"

"Yes, this. Man waves at me, friendly. He points to look at something in car. When I lean in for look... hit on head."

There ought to be a special hell for men like Perry, I thought as the knot came free and the silk, thereupon, all but unwound itself.

"Julitta," the girl said, rubbing her wrists. "My name."

I already was looking out the room's single window. "I'm Maggie." Below the window a flagstone area with stone steps led to a cellar. A jump would just about guarantee broken bones. The window itself was sealed shut by layers of paint.

"Break?" Julitta asked gesturing.

"No. The noise would bring them in here before either one of us could get out."

I made a quick search of the room, but found nothing that could be used as a weapon. Since the corpse that had been Great-Aunt Clara showed no visible cause of death, I suspected she'd been poisoned by something on the tray in front of her, but I doubted our captors could be persuaded to have a cup of tea.

A chaise longue with fringed throws draping its foot faced the door. Dropping onto the floor beside it, I dumped out my purse. The crochet hook I carried would open the lock in three or four minutes, but chances were high we'd walk directly into the arms of one of the crooks. The only other items in front of me were my wallet and badge, a pencil, lipstick and car keys, and the folding ruler I'd used in my role as efficiency expert.

If we extended the ruler and held it a few inches from the floor, we could possibly trip someone as they entered. On our knees, though, we'd make easy targets if more than one of them came in.

Julitta perched on the chaise longue, watching. My eyes scanned the room again. They came to rest on the silver tea service. Toss the cream pitcher under their feet like a ball? The handle on it would cause it to move too erratically.

Another thought occurred. I got up and began to remove things from the big silver tea tray.

"No to eat!" Julitta warned, pointing at the corpse.

"No," I agreed. I hefted the tea tray.

I'd played plenty of backyard baseball with Wee Willie and the other neighborhood kids. I usually struck out, but I swung hard.

The oval tray was heavier than a baseball bat, but it was all I had. And I thought I heard a voice in the hall.

"Get over there," I said, indicating the opposite side of the room. If bullets flew, I wanted her out of the way. The farther apart we were, the more it also improved whatever small odds I might be able to give her.

"If I can make them look at me, you run. Get out of the house. Understand?"

"Out. Yes." She nodded.

"Run to a neighbor. Tell them the old woman here is dead and there's a man with a gun."

"Old woman dead."

It was all we had time to plan. Outside the door, a key went into the lock. I stepped away from the door on my side. Julitta stepped back on hers. I took a batter's stance and prepared to swing slightly upward.

The gun hand came through the opening first, then the rest of the figure. I swung. The flat of the tray smashed into a head. A man's. Bone crunched. He dropped with a grunt.

Lena pushed in on his heels. The trim .22 in her hand pivoted in my direction, firing blindly. Reflex already had caused me to duck and raise the heavy tray in a feeble effort to shield myself.

The impact of the bullet jarred my arm as it ricocheted off the angled tray. Julitta tackled Lena and brought her down. I threw the tray at Lena's gun hand, then fell on top of her, grabbing her wrist.

Rice, whom I'd clobbered, still lay motionless. My foot hit his arm as I struggled with Lena. Then it connected with something else, the gun he'd dropped, maybe. I kicked it as hard as I could toward the side of the chaise longue where it would be out of his reach as he revived.

Lena aimed a punch at my face. It was a miracle the gun we were grappling for hadn't gone off.

"Run!" I screamed at Julitta.

"Let go of the gun and get off her, or I shoot the kid," said Perry behind me.

FIFTY

I sat up. Perry had a persuasive-looking .38 with a short barrel.

"What the hell's going on?" He was livid. "What happened to Kevin?"

"She hit him with a tray," said Lena scornfully.

"Bring him around. It was worth getting into that safe downstairs but we need to clear out."

He aimed the gun at me.

"Stay right where you are. You've made enough trouble. You." He indicated Julitta. "Sit on the floor."

"Sit," I told her, making a downward motion. It was safer for her if our captors didn't realize she understood English.

"Nick." Panic edged Lena's voice. "There's something wrong with him." She had turned Rice over and was staring at him.

"What do you mean, 'something wrong'? Is he dead?"

Our captors were probably both decent shots, Lena because she'd come from a background that numbered target shooting among its sports and Perry because he'd been a thief long enough to make it practical. What they lacked was the awareness that came as naturally as breathing to experienced thugs. Lena had forgotten Julitta and me. Even Perry had taken his eyes off me briefly.

An experienced gangster would never make such a mistake. Nor would he fail to account for every gun that had entered a room. The one I'd kicked — the one Kevin dropped — lay out of my reach beneath the chaise longue. The fringed throw hanging to the floor on the foot of the chaise hid it from the pair between me and the door.

"He's breathing, but — his eyes are open and one's rolled up funny," said Lena. "And – and he's got spittle coming out of the edge of his mouth!"

Perry nudged the other man with his toe but got no response.

"Then we only have to split the money two ways."

I scooted back an inch. He didn't notice.

"But Kevin's the only one who knew the name of the man we're supposed to meet in Detroit," Lena protested.

The forgotten gun lay six inches or more from my hand. Right behind me, however, in the things I'd dumped from my purse, was the folding ruler. Leaning on my arms, I felt for it.

"When we get there, we'll find a fence," Perry was saying.

My fingers closed on the ruler.

"Or maybe Nick here would just as soon not split the money at all," I suggested. "After all, he replaced your bracelet with a fake just like he did some of the others."

Her smirk was patronizing.

"I had mine copied two years ago. The money bought hundreds of rifles for a partisan group. When Nicky told me those Hollywood idiots were coming to the middle of nowhere, I saw a chance to help even more. America's not lifting a finger. That cow with the diamonds and all the others — none of them care! Well, *I'm* going to do what I can to save Europe!"

"Gee, that sounds noble." Shifting my weight, I began to work the ruler segments open with one hand. "Maybe you even did send money that first time." The chaise hid some of my movements. I still had to move carefully. "But stealing from Countess Szarenski along with the others? That proves you're nothing but a crook."

The paling of her face surprised me with the truth: She hadn't known.

How much of the world's evil comes from people with good intentions? Lena was helping a cause supported by tens of thousands of decent people. The difference was, she'd resorted to theft and the murder of innocent people to advance it.

Vibrating with hate, she stared at her partner in crime.

"You... good-for-nothing..."

"Relax. We'll count the money from the Poles in my half," he said blandly.

I bent the ruler segments around to form a crude lasso. With luck I could hook it around the gun and pull it toward me.

"How could you steal from someone like them? How could you, Nick?"

Julitta shifted, either because she'd understood or because she was getting impatient.

Sweet Mother Mary, don't let her move now.

My wooden lasso found the gun. It slid toward me.

"Oh, spare me your soapbox, Lena. If you want to throw away your share of what we're going to make from this on bullets and parachutes, fine. I plan to enjoy mine. It's too late to save Europe. Now grab that kid and let's—"

She shot him.

Which seemed like a good time to raise the gun my fingers had closed on and put a bullet through her shoulder.

Lena shrieked like a banshee and fell to the floor. The .22 clattered out of her hand. It discharged again.

Julitta sprang to her feet.

"Don't move, Julitta!"

Perry had doubled onto his knees, but I couldn't tell how much threat he still posed. Planting my foot in his back, I slammed him flat. It looked as though he'd been hit in the midsection. He still held his gun. His fingers were tightening. I shot his wrist. Then, very cautiously, I removed the weapon from his unresisting fingers.

When I looked up, Julitta had the gun Lena had dropped and was pointing it at her.

"Don't," I said softly. "If you shoot someone here, they'll put your father in jail. Bartoz too. Do you understand?"

It was a lie. A terrible one. But not half as bad as letting a child who'd already been through too much have another life on her conscience to wrestle with years from now.

I held my breath. My armpits were drenched. Slowly, Julitta brought the gun down to point at the floor.

Lena was bleeding profusely but wasn't injured as much as she probably thought she was. She lay on her side and alternately whimpered and cursed. I walked around to stand between her and Julitta.

"Who was the man in the flophouse, Lena? Tell me or I'll stand here and watch until you and your boyfriend both bleed to death."

"He's not my—"

"Yeah, I know. Bringing you to meet his aunt made a good excuse for you to both be here."

"He thought she'd change her will... make him her heir..."

"The man in the flophouse."

"Just some hobo, riding the trains. Kevin found him. I need a doctor—"

"What was his name?"

"I don't know!"

"You killed him and you didn't even know his name?"

"It's war! People get killed in wars!"

"There's no war here. You just didn't want to get caught."

"No! Yes. I don't know. Ohhh!"

"Why did he go to the flophouse?"

"Money. Last payment." She groaned.

"And the envelope the man left? The way he slipped out? That was just so the cops would think Tucker was spinning another tall tale if he noticed somebody had been in the safe but couldn't find anything missing, wasn't it?"

The bait Freeze had swallowed so neatly.

"Yes, yes, yes! I need—"

I turned away.

"You okay, Julitta?"

She'd come to my side.

"Yes. Okay."

Suddenly and unexpectedly a smile brightened her features.

"Name Julie is American, yes? I like."

FIFTY-ONE

Ten days later, FDR came to Dayton. Equipped with their new two-way radios, every police car in the city accompanied him in the parade.

The following afternoon, late, I stood in my office repacking my father's pipes in their canvas bag.

Business at The Canterbury had never been better, despite days of front page publicity over the robbery. My clients were happy as clams, with each other and with me. Lena was so furious at Perry that she'd told the cops every detail of what they'd done. They both would spend decades behind bars. Kevin Rice was unlikely to regain consciousness, which caused me twinges of regret now and then. The Szarenskis, Bartoz and the French artist's family had departed for Cleveland with some vague plan of starting an art gallery there.

With a last stab of uncertainty over what I was doing, I picked up the valise and headed for Finn's. Last night the pub had been jammed wall to wall with a grand celebration marking the success of the President's visit. Tonight, when I opened the door, it was as quiet as I'd expected. Only a handful of regulars were in evidence. Seamus and Connelly stood at the far end of the bar.

"Leaving town, are you?" Connelly asked as I joined them.

Seamus' eyes jumped from the bag I carried and met my own. He recognized the valise. He knew what it contained. I set it on the bar.

"Nope. I just stopped by to give you this. If you want it."

Connelly's expression grew puzzled.

"What is it?"

The tightness of my throat prevented an answer. I gestured.

"Look."

Seamus ducked his silvery head to drink some Guinness, extending us privacy. Connelly unlatched the bag. He spread its jaws. He stared, already suspecting. Lifting back the towel that wrapped the ivory-fitted blackwood pipes with their bag and bellows, he stood wordless.

His gaze rose slowly to mine. Every emotion he felt showed in it, raw and vulnerable.

"These were his, weren't they? Your da's?"

I nodded.

He swallowed, struggling to read my expression.

"You're certain about this, Maggie? There'll be no going back."

We both knew what he meant. The words stuck, but I got them out.

"I'm certain."

The End

ABOUT THE AUTHOR

M. Ruth Myers received a Shamus Award from Private Eye Writers of America for the third book in her Maggie Sullivan mysteries series. She is the author of more than a dozen books in assorted genres, some written under the name Mary Ruth Myers. She and her husband live in Ohio as domestic staff to an overly-empowered cat. They have one grown daughter.

When not writing, Ruth reads, walks and bakes. She also plays the Anglo concertina with more enthusiasm than skill. She's a fan of Irish traditional music (tunes, not songs) and of ragtime.

Get to know her better on Facebook, Twitter or Pinterest; at her blog, GalGumshoe.com; or at M.RuthMyers.com.

Made in the USA
Middletown, DE
12 September 2019